Dear Reader,

Cade and Lexi's wedding! I've been waiting for this ever since *Midnight Thunder*, book one in the Thunder Mountain Brotherhood series. I know many of you have, too! This story is tons of fun and might make you a little teary-eyed.

For those of you who are worried because you missed that first book, you'll be fine. I've put in enough trail markers so you won't get lost. Mostly you need to know that Cade and Lexi were always meant for each other but it's taken them a LONG time to get to the altar. In contrast, Austin Teague and Drew Martinelli are meeting for the first time and, although their chemistry is off the charts, they have very different visions of the future. As you might expect, that spells trouble for two lovable but conflicted people!

You'll have a chance to visit with other members of the Thunder Mountain Brotherhood, too. As you might expect, Rosie and Herb, the foster parents who gave these boys a secure home at Thunder Mountain Ranch, are beside themselves with joy at the prospect of so many of their sons returning for this epic event. Frankly, so am I. I love these guys.

Welcome back to Thunder Mountain! With a wedding coming up there's plenty going on, but Rosie is always happy to bring you a cup of coffee and fill you in on the doings. She'll even add a shot of Baileys to that coffee if you ask her real nice. Have a seat on the front porch, okay? Rosie will be along shortly!

Happily Ever After,

Vicki Lewis Thompson

Do You Take This Cowboy?

Vicki Lewis Thompson

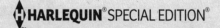

Recycling programs
for this product may
not exist in your area.

ISBN-13: 978-0-373-62364-8

Do You Take This Cowboy?

Printed in U.S.A.

A passion for travel has taken *New York Times* bestselling author **Vicki Lewis Thompson** to Europe, Great Britain, the Greek isles, Australia and New Zealand. She's visited most of North America and has her eye on South America's rain forests. Africa, India and China beckon. But her first love is her home state of Arizona, with its deserts, mountains, sunsets and—last but not least—cowboys! The wide-open spaces and heroes on horseback influence everything she writes. Connect with her at vickilewisthompson.com, Facebook.com/vickilewisthompson and Twitter.com/vickilthompson.

Books by Vicki Lewis Thompson

Harlequin Special Edition

Thunder Mountain Brotherhood

In the Cowboy's Arms
Say Yes to the Cowboy

Harlequin Blaze

Thunder Mountain Brotherhood

Midnight Thunder
Thunderstruck
Rolling Like Thunder
A Cowboy Under the Mistletoe
Cowboy All Night
Cowboy After Dark
Cowboy Untamed
Cowboy Unwrapped

Sons of Chance

Cowboys & Angels
Riding High
Riding Hard
Riding Home
A Last Chance Christmas

Visit the Author Profile page
at Harlequin.com for more titles.

To all my loyal readers who've loved the Thunder Mountain Brotherhood, thank you! Your emails and Facebook posts mean so much to me!

Chapter One

Drew Martinelli walked backward up the steps of the ranch house to the porch while keeping her camcorder focused on the couple strolling toward her hand in hand. Cade and Lexi's wedding was four days away and they'd hired Drew to create a video illustrating their love for each other, their appreciation of Thunder Mountain Ranch and their gratitude to both sets of parents. They planned to give a copy to the two couples at the rehearsal dinner as a surprise.

Because they'd wanted to shoot it at the ranch Cade grew up on, they'd had to get his foster parents, Rosie and Herb, to leave for the afternoon. They'd sent them to town on a somewhat bogus errand to pick up more decorations for the wedding. Drew knew Rosie and Herb pretty well by now. She doubted they believed the decorations were necessary but they'd played along, probably realizing something secret was going on.

Drew had begun the video down at the barn with Lexi and Cade tossing hay at each other. Next she'd followed them out to the pasture where they'd played tag with their horses, Hematite and Serendipity. She'd shot footage in the cabin where Cade had lived with two of his foster brothers as a teenager.

Then she'd walked with Cade and Lexi to their own recently constructed cabin and recorded Cade fixing lasagna. Cade's ability to cook must be a big deal because the two teased each other unmercifully during the process. Drew had struggled to keep from laughing, which would have been picked up on the mic.

A last shot on the ranch house porch would be the finale. Drew turned slowly to keep them in the frame as they climbed the steps. Cade sat in one of the roomy Adirondack chairs lining the porch and Lexi nestled on his lap.

As they'd planned, Drew crouched down and zoomed in on Lexi's face. Bits of hay stuck in her brown curls and her cheeks were flushed. Drew had a hunch Lexi's parents would totally lose it when they saw the joy and happiness in their daughter's eyes. Even Drew was a little choked up.

Lexi's warm smile completed the image. "Thank you, Mom and Dad, for always supporting me in everything I ever wanted to do and for welcoming the man I've chosen to share my life with. I love you both so much."

Drew's throat tightened. She didn't often become emotionally invested in her video subjects, but Lexi and Cade had become friends as well as clients. She slowly panned over to Cade. Wow. The big cowboy was clearly moved. That level of intensity wasn't common in the men she'd photographed.

He cleared his throat. "Mom and Dad, you took me in

when I had nowhere else to go." He cleared his throat a second time. "There's not enough thanks in the world for that. Because of you I became a man worthy of this wonderful woman. I love you more than you'll ever know."

Blinking back tears, Drew widened her camera's focus to include Cade and Lexi as they turned to each other and leaned in for a sweet, lingering kiss. Then she switched off the camera, reached for the tissue in her pocket and blew her nose.

When she looked up, Cade and Lexi were watching her in obvious bemusement.

"You got me." She tucked the tissue back in her pocket and stood. "That's one of the most touching scenes I've ever shot. Your folks are gonna turn into faucets when they see this."

"That's the idea." Lexi slid off Cade's lap.

"Yep." Cade got up and scrubbed a hand over his face. "I don't know about anybody else, but I could use a beer."

"Me, too." Lexi glanced at Drew. "Do you have time?"

"Sure, but what if Rosie and Herb come back and catch me here?"

"We'll say that you and I had more details to iron out regarding the wedding video."

"Okay, that works. Let me put my stuff in my truck."

"Oh, and you can meet Austin," Lexi said. "He's probably still working on the kitchen sink that got clogged while we were cleaning up after lunch. Thank God Austin was here or Herb would have stayed home to fix it and our plan would have been wrecked."

Cade laughed. "And we all know Herb would never have left me to do it."

"We do?" Drew looked at him. "Why not?"

"Sorry, Drew. I keep forgetting you haven't been around forever." Lexi slid her arm around Cade's waist.

"My husband-to-be has many talents but he's so not a handyman."

Cade shrugged as if he'd accepted that minor flaw long ago. "I didn't get that gene. Austin, though, he's good with tools."

"Is he the brother who just flew in from New Zealand?"

"Two days ago. Austin Teague. Nice guy." Lexi waved Drew toward her truck. "Get rid of your stuff. Your beer will be waiting for you in the kitchen."

This Austin person would be in the kitchen, too, apparently. Drew was eager to talk with someone who'd been halfway around the world, especially when he'd lived in a place she'd love to video someday.

She stashed her equipment in her truck and headed back to the house. She'd looked forward to meeting Austin ever since Rosie had mentioned him during a discussion of the wedding setup. They'd needed a head count of the foster brothers who'd be participating in the wedding.

Over the years Rosie and Herb Padgett had taken in quite a few boys, who at different times in their lives had ended up at Thunder Mountain Ranch. Cade had been one of their first foster boys, and it seemed that the whole family was excited about his wedding.

The ceremony would be held in the barn, a trendy wedding venue choice these days. But this ceremony would be unique in that the horses would remain in their stalls. Cade and Lexi were very much into horses and they loved the idea that the ranch's equine population would attend the wedding. This way Cade's cat, Ringo, could even be there if he chose.

Human guests would be seated on benches facing the barn's wide front door, which would be open. Instead of an arbor placed in the open doorway as a backdrop, the foster brothers in attendance would stand in a semicircle behind the minister.

Not all of Cade's foster brothers could make it to the wedding, but at last count at least nine would be standing in that group. Drew couldn't wait to film this ceremony, which promised to be more visually interesting than most.

She walked into the ranch house without knocking. People didn't stand on ceremony at Thunder Mountain, and while the living room was comfy and inviting, the large kitchen with its sturdy oak table was the heart of the house. She found Cade and Lexi sitting there, each with a bottle of beer. Two other open bottles were on the table along with a large bowl of chips.

Drew figured one beer was for her and the other must be for the man who was half-hidden under the kitchen sink. All she could see were scuffed boots, wear-softened jeans, a silver belt buckle with a kiwi bird etched on it, and a small section of skin that told her he was shirtless.

"Hey, Drew," Cade said. "That would be Junior's legs sticking out from under the sink over there. He says he'll be done in thirty seconds, tops."

She frowned. "Junior?"

"The name's Austin, ma'am." He wiggled partway out from under the sink, wiped his hand on his jeans and thrust it toward her. "Pleased to meet you."

"Hi, there." She walked over, leaned down and shook his outstretched hand. She tried not to stare, but *oh... my...God.* She had the urge to race back to her truck and fetch her camera. Abs and pecs like that should be captured on film and preserved for posterity. She was also amazed that he could fit those broad shoulders into such a small space.

On top of that he was blond and blue-eyed. Even his

chest hair was blond, although a little darker than the sun-bleached, close-cropped hair on his head. Because of her Italian heritage, she'd spent her life surrounded by dark-haired, dark-eyed people. She had a weakness for men who looked like Austin.

As they shook hands he smiled. "Really glad to meet you," he murmured.

"Same here." Lord help her, she sounded breathless. He probably got that a lot.

"Be done in a jiffy." He released her hand, scooted back under the sink and bumped his head on the pipe. "Ow."

"Are you okay?" She leaned down to peer into the cabinet.

"Yes, ma'am. Didn't watch where I was going is all."

"He'll be fine," Cade said. "Junior's practically indestructible."

"The name's *Austin*." His voice echoed a bit coming from under the sink.

"Why do you call him Junior?" Drew walked over to the table and Cade got up to pull out her chair.

He winked at her. "Because it's his name."

Lexi leaned over and gave him a light punch on the arm. "He's all grown up now. Retire the *Junior* thing."

"Yes, *please*," came the voice from under the sink.

"So I take it he was Junior when you all lived at the ranch?" Drew took a sip of her beer.

"And still is, as far as I'm concerned." Cade grinned as he went back to his seat. "I don't care how big he gets, he'll always be Junior to me."

"No respect." Austin slid out from under the sink and rose to his glorious height, which had to be at least six-three. "I go and sell my truck so I can buy a plane ticket to attend your wedding and this is my reward—still stuck with the same old crummy nickname." His dramatic sigh made his chest heave in a most arresting way.

"*I* call you Austin," Lexi said.

"Yes, you do, Lexi, and I appreciate the support."

Cade tipped his chair onto its back legs and picked up his beer. "The way I heard it, you didn't sell your truck to buy a plane ticket. You sold it because you wanted to buy a new one over here instead of shipping your old rattletrap across the Pacific."

"Technically, yes, but some of the proceeds went toward the ticket, so my statement stands."

"So you're staying?" Drew hadn't been clear on that but it was the best news she'd heard all day.

"Yes, ma'am. New Zealand was great, but I missed Wyoming."

"And me," Cade said. "I know you really missed me."

Austin laughed, flashing beautiful white teeth. "Can't live without you, bro."

"And FYI, your beer's getting warm the longer you stand there working your jaw."

"Let me wash up." He turned back to the sink.

Much as Drew would have loved to admire the ripple of his back muscles as he scrubbed his hands clean, ogling would be inappropriate. She redirected her attention toward Cade and Lexi. Why was she here, again? Oh, yes. "I think we got some great stuff today. I'll edit it as soon as I get home and email you a link to a preview."

"Good." Lexi reached for the chips. "I'm really excited to see it."

"So am I." Cade returned his chair to its original position so he could also reach the chip bowl. "By the way, I was impressed that you walked up the steps backward while you filmed that last part. I'm not sure I could have done that."

"I know I couldn't," Lexi said.

"My years of playing hockey probably helps. You have to have eyes in the back of your head to play that game."

"You played hockey?" Austin joined them at the table.

"Yes, and I was really, really lucky that I got to. Some parents organized a Montana youth league and my brother and I were both in it. I don't think that league exists anymore. For three years I lived and breathed hockey. Every night before I went to sleep I recited that famous Wayne Gretzky quote."

Austin picked up his beer and reached for a chip. "I don't think I know that one."

"I do, more or less," Cade said. "Instead of following the puck, you need to anticipate where it will be and go there."

"Aha!" Lexi looked as if inspiration had hit. "*That's* why you're such an excellent videographer. You're always a little ahead of the action. I couldn't put my finger on why your videos are so much better than others I've seen and I'll bet that's the secret."

Drew's cheeks warmed. "Thank you. I never thought of it that way but if I manage to pull it off I'm glad."

"Montana, huh?" Austin's gaze had remained on her ever since he'd come to the table. "Where in Montana?"

"Billings. My parents own an Italian restaurant there."

"I love Italian food. Do you like to cook?"

"God, no." She shuddered. "I'm probably the least domestic woman you'll ever meet."

"But you're great with a camera," Lexi said. "Plenty of people make videos but you make memories."

"What a lovely thing to say." Drew savored the compliment. "Any chance you'd be willing to put that in a review on my website?"

"Absolutely! I wish I'd thought of it before."

"No worries. You've been busy planning a wedding."

"Reviews make a difference," Austin said. "The company I worked for always asked for them at the end of a ride."

"Horseback ride?" Drew made a guess based on where he'd grown up.

"Yes, ma'am."

"What made you go so far away from home?" She'd done a little bit of traveling related to her videography but she'd never considered relocating to a different country. His willingness to seek out adventure added to his appeal.

"*Lord of the Rings*. When I saw those movies I stayed for the credits. That's when I made up my mind I had to go to New Zealand." He popped another chip in his mouth.

"How old were you?"

"I must've been around thirteen."

Cade nodded. "Oh, yeah, you were thirteen, all right. I remember it well. You drove us all crazy with your fixation on those movies and New Zealand." He looked at Drew. "Watch out for Junior. Once he gets an idea in his head, he's like one of those bullet trains in Japan."

"That's not such a bad thing." Drew sent Austin a glance of solidarity. "Nothing wrong with being highly motivated to attain a goal."

He tipped his head in silent acknowledgment.

"True," Cade said. "But if you've booked a seat on that train you'd better be sure you want to go where it's headed." He looked over at Austin. "I'm flattered that you came back for the wedding, but surely you have other reasons for relocating to your old stomping grounds. At least I hope you do. I can only be entertaining for so long before I run out of material."

Austin rotated his bottle on the table and smiled at Cade. "The new truck's a clue, bro."

Cade gazed at him and then he blinked. "I'll be damned. I should have figured that out."

Lexi turned to Drew. "I have no idea what they're talking about, do you?"

"No." But she was intrigued. Austin was clearly a man who knew what he wanted and went after it. He hadn't allowed the ties to his foster parents or his foster brothers to stop him from pursuing a dream that had taken him halfway around the world.

She, on the other hand, had felt obligated to stay in Billings far too long. She was the oldest and her large family seemed to depend on her for support and advice. But in the past year or so she'd felt smothered by their neediness. She'd been desperate to get away and discover who she was outside of that boisterous clan.

Over the Christmas holiday she'd talked her way into teaching a six-week course in videography at Sheridan's community college. That had justified moving her base of operations from Billings to Wyoming in January.

Through Molly Radcliffe, who worked at the college and was Cade's cousin, she'd met Rosie and Herb. That connection had brought her business and friendship. Today it had brought her in contact with Austin. He probably had something to teach her about making bold moves toward an exciting future.

It sounded as if he had a grand plan for his decision to come back home. That put him several steps ahead of her. As of now, she was making it up as she went along.

She knew what she didn't want—to be dragged down by so many family obligations that she lost track of her own goals and who she was besides oldest daughter and big sister. Austin had already made that journey away from his people. Maybe hanging out with him would give her the gumption she needed to do the same. And whether his spirit of adventure rubbed off or not, he was pretty to look at.

"So why is the truck a clue to your current plans?" Lexi asked.

Austin hesitated and exchanged a quick glance with Cade.

Cade flashed him a smile. "You're the one who said it."

Austin cleared his throat and faced Lexi. "Well, a man who's starting out fresh needs a decent ride to…to…" He sent Cade a look that was clearly a plea for a little help with this explanation.

"A man's truck is like his alter ego," Cade said. "You can tell a lot by what he chooses to drive. Junior, here, is ready to project a more polished image."

Austin let out a relieved sigh. "Exactly."

Drew figured it was a guy thing. She didn't care what Austin chose to drive. She just wanted to be in the passenger seat.

Chapter Two

Drew left far sooner than Austin would have liked, but she had to get home and edit the video and he was all in favor of that. He wanted her to finish it because he had other plans for how she'd spend her evening, assuming she wasn't seeing anyone. When he'd first slid out from under that sink, he felt as if he'd been struck by lightning.

The view from the floor had been spectacular—long, tanned legs that ended in a snug pair of jeans shorts and above that a bare, toned midriff and a white halter top that had gaped a little when she'd leaned over to shake his hand.

But he hadn't focused on that because he was a gentleman. Instead he'd gazed into eyes that were a beautiful deep brown and gleamed with interest. Excellent. Mutual attraction.

She wore a silver pendant consisting of a freeform heart, a large pearl and several little diamonds. He'd no-

ticed it because it had swung toward him when she'd bent
down. It looked expensive, and yet she'd worn it when
she was dressed very casually. That interested him, too.

He munched on chips and sipped his beer while Cade
and Lexi discussed the video they'd just made and how
awesome it was going to be. When he heard Drew's truck
pull away, he turned to Lexi. "Does she have a steady
guy?"

Cade sighed. "Look out. Bullet train."

"Not necessarily." Austin sat up a little straighter. "She
seemed interested in me. It might go nowhere, but what's
wrong with checking things out if she's available?"

"I don't think she's with anyone," Lexi said. "When
I asked if she wanted to bring a guest to the wedding
she said no."

"That's great." He got up and retrieved his phone from
where he'd laid it on the kitchen counter. "I'd like her
number." He settled back in his chair and clicked on his
contacts page. "What's her last name?"

"Martinelli." Lexi took out her phone.

"That explains the big brown eyes and the Italian restaurant." He typed in her name. "Ready when you are."

Cade tugged his hat down over his eyes and groaned.
"If you give him that number, I guarantee he'll dial it
right now."

"So what?" Lexi scrolled through her contacts. "If she
doesn't want to go out with him she can always say no."

Leaning both elbows on the table, Cade studied Austin. "When are you fixing to get that courtin' truck?"

"That *what*?" Lexi looked up from her phone. "Is a
courtin' truck what I think it is?"

"Yes, ma'am." Cade took a long pull on his beer.

She turned to Austin. "Are you really buying a new
truck so you can impress women?"

"Not *all* women. Just certain ones."

"Let me put it this way, Lexi." Cade put down his beer. "When you attended that riding clinic in Denver last year you took cabs to get around, right?"

"Right."

"How did you know a cab was available?"

"The roof light was on."

"Well, Junior here has his light on."

"I do not." Austin glared at his brother. "That suggests I'll take the first one who comes along, and that's not how I—"

"Isn't Drew the first one who's come along?"

"Yes, but we still don't know if she'll go out with me."

"What if she does?"

"Then I'll have to go truck shopping pretty soon."

"Wait, wait, wait." Lexi waved her hands in the air. "You two are speaking in tongues. Could you both use your native language, which also happens to be mine? What the hell are you talking about?"

Cade reached over and covered her hand with his. "I called it his courtin' truck because Junior is looking for a wife."

Lexi swiveled in her seat to look at Austin. "You are?"

He hadn't planned to lay out his plan this soon but he also couldn't beat around the bush with Lexi. She was like a big sister to him. "Yes, ma'am."

"See?" Cade gestured to him. "I knew he had another reason for coming back to Wyoming besides our wedding."

"Austin." Lexi put her hand on his arm. "Please tell me you didn't get this idea because of our wedding invitation. There's such a thing as wedding fever. When I was twenty-two I tried to get Cade to propose because of peer pressure. You probably don't remember that."

"Oh, I remember, all right. That's when he took off for Colorado." At seventeen, Austin had been devastated when his idol had driven away from Thunder Mountain Ranch. Lexi hadn't been the only one with a broken heart. "It wasn't just the invitation, although that made me realize all I was missing and I didn't want to miss this. But I've been thinking about moving back and settling down for quite a while now."

"You're only twenty-six. You have lots of time."

"I know. The thing is, I'm sick of getting involved with someone when it'll never go anywhere. Every woman I dated in New Zealand told me flat out she wasn't relocating. That made perfect sense. Their families were there and it's a beautiful country."

"All right." Lexi seemed relieved. "Then *ultimately* you want to get married, but you don't have a timetable or anything." She smiled. "It's not like you'll ask Drew out now and propose next week."

"I certainly wouldn't plan on it."

"Good, because—"

"But what if she's perfect? What if we're perfect for each other? Life's short. We don't know what's going to happen." He'd learned that early. Both his parents had died in their thirties. "I don't believe in putting things off if taking action is the right decision."

Cade glanced up at the ceiling.

Austin knew he didn't fully agree, but Drew had liked that he was focused. Didn't mean she'd go out with him but he thought she would. He didn't get many refusals when he asked a lady out.

He glanced at the phone in Lexi's free hand. "So can I have the number?"

She looked at him for a moment longer. "Yes. Just—"

"Just what?"

"Nothing." She squeezed his arm and moved her hand away. "Ready?"

He touched the screen to refresh it. "Yes, ma'am." He entered Drew's number. "Do you think she's had time to get home?"

"Probably not."

"Then I'll wait." He put down his phone and picked up his beer. "It sounded like you were both happy with how the filming went."

"I think it went great," Lexi said. "I'll know for sure once we see the edited version, but I meant what I said about her work. She's phenomenal."

"Good to know. Now that I understand how to run a trail ride company, I've been thinking about starting one. A good video on a website would be a big help."

Cade leaned forward. "Gonna go into business for yourself?"

"I'd like to. I'll have to begin small, work with one of the local stables, maybe get a business loan, but I think that's all doable."

"Absolutely," Lexi said. "I'm sure Rosie and Herb would let you stay here for a while, which would save money on rent."

Austin had been thinking the same thing until meeting Drew. "They probably would and I've considered it, but I'd rather get an apartment in town."

Cade gave him a knowing look. "That doesn't surprise me. I—" He paused as the front door opened.

"Anybody home?"

"Hey, Zeke!" Cade pushed back his chair. "We're in the kitchen having a beer. Come on back and I'll get you one."

"Don't mind if I do."

Austin left his chair to greet his foster brother, one

he'd liked okay but had never felt close to when they'd all lived at Thunder Mountain. Zeke Rafferty had kept to himself and all the guys had figured it was because his dad had committed suicide. But Rosie said that Zeke had come out of his shell ever since discovering he was about to be a father.

It seemed that Rosie was right, because the rugged cowboy who'd always looked slightly ticked off came in all smiles. "Hey, Austin!" His handshake was firm and enthusiastic. "I swear you're a lot taller than I remember."

"Not much taller, but I filled out a little."

"I'd say so. How was New Zealand?" He took the beer Cade handed him. "Thanks, bro."

"I loved New Zealand but I got homesick."

Zeke nodded. "I can understand that. New Zealand's a long way from Wyoming. Listen, I came over hoping you'd be around. As you've probably heard, I've been the caretaker at Matt's ranch for the past few weeks."

"I did hear that." Their foster brother Matt Forrest was starring in his first major film and he'd used the sudden influx of money to buy a ranch adjoining Thunder Mountain. "Matt's premiere was another reason to come back. I want to go to LA with everybody next month."

"Yeah, with all the people going, we might end up renting a couple of vans instead of flying. Anyway, my situation is changing and I'm looking for someone to take over for me at Matt's. I thought you might be interested."

"That could be a good deal for you, Junior," Cade said. "Free room and board."

Austin thought about it for less than two seconds. Good deal or not, it would mean he'd agreed to take care of someone else's place instead of moving toward buying his own. He might have to start with a tiny apartment, but it would be his. Paying his rent on time would establish his creditworthiness when he applied for a home loan.

He gazed at Zeke. "Much as I'd like to help, staying at Matt's doesn't fit in with my plans. Sorry." He noticed that Lexi and Cade exchanged a look. At one time he would have followed any advice either of them had given him. But he'd had four years of being completely on his own. He still respected their opinions, but he no longer felt obligated to make decisions based on what they thought.

"That's okay." Zeke shrugged. "Just thought I'd ask." He moved to the table and took a seat. "Somebody will turn up."

"They will." Cade walked to the refrigerator. "Who's ready for another beer? Junior?"

"In a little while, thanks. If you'll all excuse me, I need to make a phone call." He left the kitchen and walked through the living room and out to the porch. Now that the moment was here, he had to decide where he'd take Drew if she agreed to go out with him.

Then it came to him. Plopping into an Adirondack chair, he touched the screen and put the phone to his ear. Damn it, he got her voice mail. "Hi, this is Austin Teague. I enjoyed meeting you today and was hoping you'd have some free time tonight." He gave his number and disconnected.

He knew she was going home because she had a video to edit, so she might have been engrossed in that and hadn't heard the phone. Or maybe she automatically let every call go to voice mail. Then again, she might have turned off her phone. She might—

His phone chimed and her name popped up on the screen. Heart pounding, he answered. "Hi, Drew."

"Hi, yourself." She sounded happy. Interested. "Didn't expect to hear from you so soon."

"Didn't you?"

"Well, okay, I sort of did. What did you have in mind?"

He didn't dare tell her what was in his mind this very minute. He'd already started imagining what it would be like to kiss her.

"Austin? Are you there?"

"Yes, ma'am. Sorry. I'm on the porch and got distracted by…" He glanced around for an excuse. "A butterfly."

"I can understand how that could happen. They're beautiful, aren't they?"

"Yes, ma'am. Anyway, here's my thought, if you're available for dinner. We'll have a cookout."

"Where?"

"There's a nice little spot on a far corner of the ranch property. Since you're not into cooking, I'll handle that."

"Sounds like fun."

"I can pick you up."

"That's totally unnecessary. I'll meet you there. What time?"

He glanced at the time on his phone and quickly calculated how long he'd need to set things up. "Is seven too late?"

"Seven's perfect. That will give me time to finish the video and send the link to Cade and Lexi. I'll see you then."

"Great!" He disconnected the call. He'd just given himself a heck of a lot of work to do in a short time. This was his deal so he wouldn't raid the Thunder Mountain kitchen for what he needed.

But he had a transportation problem. His foster mom and dad had been generous with the loan of their truck but they weren't back from town. He really did need to buy that courtin' truck Cade had teased him about, but he certainly wouldn't be doing that between now and seven tonight.

As if in answer to his silent plea, Herb and Rosie drove up and parked in front of the porch steps. Austin got up and went around to the passenger side where Rosie was to see if he could help with her packages.

His foster mom was a short, rounded lady who had decided to be a blond for the rest of her life. She was the kindest woman Austin had ever known, but tough enough to keep her foster boys in line. Most of the time there had been at least ten boys living in the log cabins down in the meadow. They'd all known that Rosie was the boss around here.

She'd already opened her door but he was able to take her shopping bags and give her a hand down. She was perfectly capable of doing all that herself, but she'd taught her boys to be gentlemen. They'd practiced their manners on her because usually she'd been the only available woman.

"Are you the sentry?" she asked as she stepped down from the truck's running board.

"The sentry?"

"You know. The lookout. The person watching for us in case we got home before whatever was happening was still happening."

"Oh. No, ma'am." Then he realized he hadn't contradicted her assumption that something secret was going on. "I mean, nothing's happening. Nothing at all. Zeke's inside talking to Cade and Lexi. That's about the size of it."

"I saw Zeke's truck parked down by the barn." Herb, a wiry man who'd finally surrendered to wearing glasses in his later years, chuckled as he walked around the truck to join them. "We dawdled in town as long as we could but finally ran out of things to do other than cruising Main Street. That looks a little strange for a couple of sixtysomethings."

"Like I said." Austin tried to blot out the image of Drew because she was part of the secret. "Not a single thing going on, except the sink's fixed."

"Thank you!" Rosie beamed at him. "By the way, now that some of my boys are back, they sometimes get together for poker. If they ask you to play, you might want to think twice."

"Yes, ma'am, I already know I'm lousy at poker. Some of the guides got me into a game and ended up with all my tip money for the week."

"I'm sorry to hear that. But at least now you know it's not your thing."

"Nothing wrong with being a bad liar, son." Herb clapped him on the shoulder. "So are you saying it's okay for us to go in the house?"

"Absolutely. But now that you're back, would it be possible for me to borrow the truck to run a few errands?"

"Sure thing." Herb handed over the keys.

"And would it be okay if I used a Coleman stove for a little cookout on the back twenty tonight? I'll get the food, but I'll also need to borrow some tongs and a pan or two."

Rosie smiled at him. "This sounds like it could be a date."

"It is." And now he was in the soup because she'd probably ask who he'd asked out and how he could possibly have met someone when he'd been in town exactly two days. He was saved when Zeke, Cade and Lexi came out the front door.

Amid much laughter and teasing, Rosie and Herb

promised they wouldn't try to uncover whatever surprise was in the works. Lexi wanted to see what they'd bought in town so Austin handed her the bags and excused himself to go put on a shirt. That finished, he grabbed his hat and wallet and headed out the door, his shirt still unbuttoned. He was eager to get away before he had to answer any more questions that would bring up the subject of Drew being here.

But Lexi had to call out to him. "Does this mean she said yes?"

"She did."

Rosie lifted her eyebrows. "So who's the lucky lady?"

"I'll let Lexi explain it." Touching his fingers to the brim of his hat, he hurried around the truck, hopped in and made his escape.

Chapter Three

Drew pulled into the ranch's circular gravel drive exactly at seven. The sun had dipped behind the Bighorn Mountains, but there was still plenty of light to see Austin sitting on the porch in one of the Adirondack chairs. The picture he made in his gray Stetson, yoked Western shirt, boots and faded jeans was exactly why so many women fantasized about cowboys.

That outfit, especially on a man built like Austin, made her feel safe. Like the knights of old, he would leap on his horse and ride to her rescue. Even though she didn't need rescuing, she still loved the idea of a cowboy hero who'd protect her from the bad guys and look great doing it.

He left his chair as she shut off the motor. Anticipation thrummed through her veins as he came down the steps with the slightly bowlegged stride common to men who'd spent most of their lives on horseback. Oddly enough, she hadn't dated cowboys while living in Montana.

In high school and college she'd hung out with the art students and at home her life had revolved around the family restaurant. She'd dated some artist types and a couple of chefs but no cowboys. Thunder Mountain, however, was chockablock with them.

She moved her purse to the floor of the passenger side out of habit. Nobody would break into her truck to steal it while she was parked here. She tossed the keys down there, too, and opened her door. She'd started to climb out when he rounded the front of the vehicle.

"Let me help you down."

Amused, she waited. She couldn't remember the last time someone had made that offer. He knew perfectly well she was capable of getting down by herself. But when he held out his hand, she was charmed.

"I like your hair like that."

"Thanks." Most of the summer she'd worn it in a braid or a ponytail but she'd decided to leave it down tonight. She was on a date, after all.

"I'm glad you could make it."

"Me, too." She put her hand in his and the controlled strength in his grip sent a shiver of pleasure up her arm. "Fortunately the editing went well and I had time to finish the video." Then she glanced around, not sure who might be within hearing distance. "Did you have to dream up a story to explain to your folks how we ended up going out tonight?"

"I have Lexi to thank for that. She told them you came out today to check on some details for the wedding video." He let go of her hand once she had both feet on the ground.

"That will give them another hint, though." She breathed in the scent of his aftershave. "They know something's going on."

He sighed. "You're right. Now they might think it involves a video. My mistake. If we'd met in town I could've snuck away without explaining I was meeting someone."

"I didn't think of that, either, so I'm as much at fault as you." Something else occurred to her but when she gazed into his blue eyes she lost her train of thought.

He smiled. "Not letting you shoulder any of the blame, ma'am. I complicated things, case closed."

Ah, that smile. And speaking of shoulders…

She remembered what she'd been about to say. "Actually, Lexi took a risk when she invited me in for a beer. When I pointed out that Rosie and Herb might come back and find me there, she came up with that cover story she used to help you out."

"Yeah?" He brightened. "I didn't know that."

"And if she hadn't invited me in for a beer, you and I wouldn't have met."

"So it's all Lexi's fault?"

She laughed. "Pretty much."

"Now I don't feel so guilty. I just thought a cookout would be more fun than a boring restaurant meal."

"You've got that right. I was thrilled with the suggestion. I've spent so much time in Martinelli's that I don't care if I never eat in another restaurant again."

"Then I'm glad I thought of it."

"So where are we headed? Backyard barbecue? Fire pit?"

He gestured toward the edge of the porch. "We'll take the ATV out to the back twenty."

She looked and sure enough, a green-and-brown ATV was sitting there. She'd been so focused on his handsome self she hadn't noticed it. "The back twenty? I've only heard people refer to the back forty."

"They do." He started walking toward the ATV. "But this ranch isn't that big so we have the back twenty. We joke about it, but I have great memories of the place. It's where we used to camp out when we were kids. Or I should say, when I was a kid and was allowed to tag along with the big guys. I came here when I was nine. Everybody else was a teenager."

"And so they called you Junior."

"Mostly Cade." He stopped next to the ATV and turned to her with another one of his endearing smiles. "I don't mind it as much as he thinks I do. I did back then, but now…now I think he says it because he likes me."

"I'm pretty sure he likes you." She wondered if Austin had any idea how appealing he was. "Cade strikes me as the kind of guy who only teases people he likes."

He nodded. "These days, probably so. But you should have heard the way he said *Junior* years ago when I used to bug him to death. I followed him everywhere. Looking back on it, I wonder why he didn't deck me. I'll bet he wanted to but I was a lot smaller and he'd never have beat up on someone smaller."

"Then he must like you, because you've grown enough for him to beat up on if he wanted to."

"Guess so." He laughed. "Come to think of it, yesterday he said now I was too big to mess with, especially since he's hit thirty and is losing muscle mass."

"So if he's thirty, how old are you?"

"Twenty-six."

"Huh." She decided to go for full disclosure and get it over with. "How do you feel about having a cookout with an older woman?"

"I don't care how old you are."

"For the record, I'm twenty-eight."

He shrugged. "Two years is nothing." He turned toward

the ATV, but then swung back to her. "Unless you're not happy about going out with a younger guy. Some ladies would rather date someone older than they are. I've run into a few of those."

Silly women. "I'm not one of them."

"Good to know." He swung one long leg over the ATV. "Climb on behind me and we'll get this show started. Oh, and hold on tight. I won't be going fast but we'll hit some bumps along the way. Can't help it. The rain's done a number on the road."

She needed no encouragement to wrap both arms around his solid torso and scoot against his firm backside. Riding on the back of an ATV with Austin immediately became her favorite outdoor activity. What a great excuse to get up close and personal with a guy who not only looked good but felt even better.

The ride ended long before she was ready to let go of him. He pulled into a clearing with a boundary marked by rocks spaced a few inches apart. Beyond them the brush, mostly sage, grew three to four feet high.

But now they'd stopped and she felt obliged to climb off, darn it. She had a nice buzz going and she had the crazy urge to ask if that had been as good for him as it had been for her.

When he just sat there while he took a couple of deep breaths, she had a feeling it had been.

"Lordy." His low chuckle was followed by a long sigh. "Maybe I should have taken you to a restaurant in town, after all."

"Oh?"

"I knew I was attracted to you, but I thought I could manage a short ATV ride. Turns out it affected me more than I thought it would." He climbed off the four-wheeler and faced her. "But everything's under control now." He gave her a sheepish smile. "I promise you're safe with me."

She met his gaze. "If it makes you feel any better, the drive turned me on, too."

Heat flared in his eyes.

She felt obliged to add one more fact. "But we just met."

"Only hours ago."

"At this point it wouldn't be about you and me as individuals with histories and personality quirks. It would be like strangers scratching an itch. Not that there's anything wrong with that, but I—"

"I didn't invite you out here to scratch an itch. I'm past that stage in my life."

"Good. So am I. Come to think of it, I never went through that stage." She noticed a folded blanket on top of a metal ice chest but that was probably so they'd have a place to sit. "I've always wanted to get to know someone first."

"Exactly."

"It's good we're agreed on that." Definitely good. Maybe. Except he wasn't some guy she'd met in a bar. She knew his foster family. She knew he'd been to New Zealand. She knew he could fix a clogged sink. "I see you've toted everything out here already, so let's have our meal and swap stories."

"That was my plan." He gestured toward the campsite he'd set up. "Welcome to our dining room. That little fire pit is strictly for ambiance. I'm using the Coleman stove to make dinner. Cooking over a campfire gives you lots of atmosphere but it can also give you undercooked or overcooked food."

"A Coleman stove sounds fine. I have one myself."

"You do? I thought you didn't cook."

"I don't when I have alternatives, but I camp out quite a bit when I'm shooting nature videos. I love my coffee in the morning and scrambled eggs are nice to go with it. What can I do to help?"

"The cooking's my deal, but you can light the camp-fire if you want. I left some matches next to it."

"Looks like you thought of everything." She walked over and crouched next to the fire pit where he'd arranged kindling and a couple of larger logs. Extra wood was stacked nearby. She recognized a fire laid by someone who knew what he was doing and sure enough, it caught with one match. "Done."

"Then all you have to do is keep an eye on it and add a log if you think it needs one. You can have a seat on the blanket and I'll get you something to drink."

"I won't object to that." She found a good spot for the blanket, folded it so two could fit and sat down. The clearing had been raked recently but she'd guess the rocks defining the perimeter had been there for years.

"You know what?" He opened the ice chest. "I should have asked you about the wine instead of making an assumption because you're Italian."

"You brought Chianti."

"No, I brought a New Zealand Sauvignon Blanc." He held it up. "The assumption was that you were a wine drinker. Like I said, I should have asked."

"I am a wine drinker and I'm glad it's not Chianti. I can have that anytime just by walking in the back door of Martinelli's and asking for a glass."

"All righty, then." He twisted off the screw top. "It was going to be this or water. I didn't bring anything else to drink." He took out two chilled glasses and handed her one. "I had this when I was over there and really liked it." He poured them each some wine.

"I'm sure I will, too." She lifted her glass in his direction. "Here's to adventure."

"To adventure." He tapped his glass to hers. "That's a good thing to toast."

"I haven't had nearly as much adventure as you, I'm afraid." She took a slow sip. "Nice wine."

"Then I lucked out. Here's hoping the meal works for you, too."

"Since I rarely cook, almost any food made by someone else works for me."

"This is a skillet dish a trail guide buddy created." Setting his wine on the ground beside him, he hunkered down, turned on the stove and began pulling ingredients out of the ice chest. "It's flexible regarding ingredients. Some kind of white fish, vegetables you have on hand and rice."

"Sounds gourmet."

"My friend's a talented guy. Once every two weeks we offered an overnight trail ride. He was the chef on those outings."

"I'm betting you were in charge of the fire."

"Yes, ma'am."

Drew savored her wine. "Your life over there seems exotic and wonderful. I'm a little surprised you didn't stay."

"I wanted to spend enough time there that I felt the rhythm of the place in my bones." He tended his stir-fry dinner. "But I always knew I'd come back here."

"I like that idea—absorbing a place until you feel the rhythm in your bones. That's what I try to do when I shoot a video. I think I'm almost there with Thunder Mountain." She took another swallow of wine. "You're a bit of a philosopher, aren't you?"

"I don't know about that, but ever since I saw *The Lord*

of the Rings I've been into books. I might've read that phrase somewhere so don't give me too much credit."

"What books?"

"Anything about adventure, courage, honor, stuff like that. A librarian steered me toward *The Iliad* and *The Odyssey.* If I'd known that was serious literature I never would have read them. I'd taken enough teasing for *Lord of the Rings.*"

"But you liked them?"

"Sure did." He paused to drink some wine. "My dad was kind of an epic hero. That's probably why I related to those stories."

She went very still. She knew this was important information but she didn't know how to get him to elaborate. Finally, she decided to make it simple. "Would you tell me about your dad?"

His answer was slow in coming, but at last he spoke. "He was in Search and Rescue."

She slowly let out her breath and waited for the story to unfold.

"A minor avalanche had trapped a family of five. My dad was on the team that went in to get them out." He kept his attention on his cooking, carefully stirring the mixture in the pan. "They rescued everyone except the family dog. My dad went back for the dog and a second avalanche hit. The dog jumped out of his arms when he saw his family and ran to them. But when he jumped, he threw my dad off balance. He couldn't get up fast enough."

"That's rough."

He switched off the burner and put a lid on the pan. "It was rough, especially because I was only six and idolized him." Standing, he reached into a basket next to the cooler and took out plates, napkins and utensils.

"My mom must have been torn apart by the news, but she said all the right things to me—that my dad had died doing what he loved and he'd helped save the family and their beloved pet."

She wanted to hug him and offer comfort, even though the event had taken place twenty years ago. Didn't matter. He still felt the loss. She could tell by the catch in his voice as he'd finished the story.

But their relationship was still so new that she hesitated. At least she could help with serving up the meal. She got to her feet. "I'll hold the plates while you fill them."

"Good idea." He handed her the dishes with the silverware and napkins on top. As he met her gaze, his voice gentled. "I know it seems like I got a rotten deal, but compared to the other foster boys, I was lucky. My parents adored each other and adored me. I thank God for that every day."

That was when she realized she only had half the story. His dad died when he was six and he'd come to the ranch when he was nine. She asked the question as gently as possible. "And your mom?"

"She was a riding teacher. A normally steady horse freaked out. She fell off, broke her neck and died instantly."

"Oh, Austin."

"I'm not saying it wasn't awful, because it was. But after my dad died she spent the next three years emphasizing that I should do what I love because nobody knows the future. She loved riding almost as much as she loved me."

"So you went to New Zealand."

"Yes, ma'am. I knew they would have wanted me to."

"Well, then." She managed to give him a smile. "I can't wait to see what adventure you choose next."

He smiled back. "Who knows? You might want to be a part of it."

"You know, I just might."

Chapter Four

As dusk arrived along with a cool breeze, Austin decided they should sit closer to the fire while they ate. He switched on the lantern he'd brought but kept it on low to preserve the ambience. As he settled down next to Drew on the blanket, he could feel the hum of sexual tension moving back through his system.

He did his best to ignore it and tucked into the stir-fry. It had turned out fairly well, which was a relief. Multitasking had never been one of his favorite ways to operate and he wouldn't have chosen to cook dinner while telling his life story. But he'd known those facts had to come out, and the sooner the better. If he expected to spend more time with Drew, she needed to hear about his folks.

But he wanted to know her story, too. She'd worn the pearl-and-diamond pendant again tonight with a long-sleeved cotton shirt and jeans. Clearly it was important to her, so he decided to start with that. He mentioned that he'd noticed it when they'd first met.

She glanced down at the pendant as if she'd forgotten it was there. "My grandmother gave it to me for my sixteenth birthday."

"You had it on earlier today, too." Her scent, light and sweet, mingled with the aroma of wood smoke from the fire. It was an arousing combination.

"I wear it every day. I didn't use to, though." She picked up her wineglass and drank what was left in it.

"More?" He reached for the bottle.

"Sure."

"Might as well finish off the bottle." He divided the rest between them. "So when did you start wearing it all the time?"

"After she died last October. Wearing it makes me feel close to her again."

"Ah." He should have guessed something like that. "I'm sorry."

She put down her fork and looked over at him. "Me, too, but she was ninety-three and wasn't well. I miss her like crazy, but that's all about me. She was ready."

"Ninety-three. That's a good run." He wondered if she realized she was now holding on to the pendant and moving it slowly back and forth along its chain.

"She had a full life, although not one I would have chosen. My mother was the youngest of nine children."

"Whew."

"I know. My mom has a framed picture of my grandparents surrounded by all those kids. I would have gone insane with a brood like that depending on me, constantly needing things, but in the picture she looks serene. That's something I admired about her. Our family is huge and when we all get together it's a circus. Nonna Elena took it all in stride."

"Rosie's like that. Growing up, there could've been

ten or eleven of us running around, more if we'd invited our friends over, and she hardly ever lost her cool. When she needed us to behave, though, all she had to do was give us The Look."

Drew smiled. "Nonna Elena had that technique down, too. We used to say she could cut glass with The Look."

"How many of that crew lives in Billings?"

"Most of them." She let go of the pendant, picked up her fork and went back to her meal. "Did I remember to tell you this is really good? I've been so busy eating it I might not have."

"Since you weren't gagging and choking, I figured you were okay with it. Save room for dessert, though. I bought brownies at the bakery while I was in town." He noticed she'd changed the subject. Was that on purpose?

"I love brownies, but I want to finish this, which means I'll be too full for dessert. Can we wait awhile?"

"Yes, ma'am. I'm flattered you like the stir-fry so much."

"It's great."

"Want the recipe?" He grinned at her.

"How about I just talk you into making it for me again sometime?"

"Love to."

"I look forward to it." She went back to eating.

He did, too, but he wanted to find out if the change of subject had been deliberate. "Do you miss living close to your family?"

She finished chewing and swallowed. "Sometimes, I guess." Then she shook her head. "At the risk of sounding awful, no, I don't really miss that. If we were in Billings right now, I could expect several texts tonight wanting info about my date. I'm thrilled that they don't even know you exist."

"Gonna keep me a secret?" He finished off his meal and set aside his plate.

"For now, if you don't mind. I love them all and they love me, but we're too enmeshed, at least in my estimation. I came to Sheridan to escape the lack of privacy and the constant expectations."

"A lot of privacy out here." Seductive privacy that was working on him the longer they sat within inches of each other. By turning his head a fraction, he could study her profile—her high, intelligent forehead, thick dark lashes, prominent cheekbones and plump lips, which he'd longed to taste ever since he'd had his first glimpse of them while lying under the sink.

"Yes, I like this a lot. Much better than a crowded restaurant." She scooped up her last bite and ate it.

"And no obligations."

She put down her plate and gazed at him. "I like that a lot, too."

"For example, just because I brought you out here to this extremely secluded place, fed you a good dinner and served you some excellent wine, you're not obliged to kiss me."

Her full mouth widened in a smile. "Really?"

"Scout's honor. And that's legit because I was a Boy Scout."

"That doesn't surprise me at all. Okay, then I'll point out that just because I showered, changed clothes and drove out here to meet you when I could have spent the evening watching a movie in my grubby old sweats, you're not obliged to kiss me, either."

"Now that's where you're wrong." He laid his hat on the blanket before reaching out to cup her cheek. Her skin felt so delicate that he lightened his touch. "I have a huge obligation after you made all those sacrifices." He rubbed his thumb gently over skin soft as a rose petal.

Her breath hitched. "It was nothing."

"That's not the way I heard it." He leaned closer and watched her eyes flutter closed and her lips part in invitation. "Sounds to me like you went to a lot of trouble to be here."

"On second thought, maybe I did."

"Let me make it up to you." His heart thundered as he brushed his mouth over her velvet lips. He could barely feel her hand as she slipped it around his neck, yet knowing she'd reached for him heated his blood.

He moaned and fit his lips to hers, pressing a little, then a little more. Her grip on his neck tightened a tiny bit. Slowly he began to explore with his tongue, savoring the warm, arousing taste of her. Her jaw slackened ever so slightly. Easy, easy...

Drawing back, he changed the angle, settling down more firmly this time and becoming bolder with his tongue. A tiny whimper, a quick gasp, and she surrendered completely, opening to him with a rush of passion that made him dizzy.

He rose to his knees and cradled her face in both hands. She mirrored him, gripping his shoulders as she balanced on her knees and turned fully into his kiss, her intensity matching his.

Breathing hard, he lifted his head. "We should probably—"

"I know." She gulped for air and leaned back, but she didn't let go of him. "This is crazy."

"Feels good, though."

"It does, but..." She closed her eyes and shook her head. "I think—" She sucked in a breath and let it out again. "I think we need to slow down."

"Agreed." He reminded himself he was in this for the long haul. He combed his fingers through her silky hair and resisted the urge to grip her head and kiss her again. "We met a few hours ago."

Letting go of him, she took another deep breath and settled back on her heels. "We'll deal with this sudden attraction like two intelligent adults."

"One intelligent adult. All my brain cells are swimming in testosterone right now so I don't qualify." But one thought did make it through his fevered brain. "I'm buying a truck tomorrow."

She stared at him. *"What?"*

"I'll have my own truck by tomorrow afternoon." He retrieved his hat and put it on.

"What's having your own truck got to do with anything?"

"It's a guy thing. I don't want to borrow the ranch truck every time we go out. Which reminds me. Are you free tomorrow night?" He sat back and winced at the sharp pinch of unforgiving denim on his privates.

"No, I'm not. I'll be camping at the Pryor Mountain Wild Horse Refuge so I can get more video of the mustangs."

"Oh." He hesitated. Asking her to change her plans seemed pushy, even for a guy who liked to seize the moment. "I've heard about that place. Never been out there, though. Sounds interesting." Maybe she'd agree to put it off. Tomorrow night was his window of opportunity because the following night was Cade's bachelor party. Then they were into the weekend wedding activities with the rehearsal Friday and the wedding Saturday.

"It's fascinating out there. I have a friend who works at the center and she keeps me posted on the herd's activities. Right now the horses are hanging out in an ideal location for the kind of footage I'm looking for."

"You probably need to grab that opportunity while you can." His chances of spending an evening with her anytime soon were growing dimmer by the minute.

"Right. I would have gone this afternoon except Lexi and Cade asked me to film the video for their folks and it had to be edited right away. I like to get out there in the late afternoon and set up camp, so I couldn't see that working out today."

"So how about this. What if I went with you?" It was a bold suggestion, but tough times called for tough measures.

She blinked. "Um, I'll be camping overnight."

"So you'd rather not?" He didn't want to push her. "Look, I realize that might not work for you. Like we've said, we just met." He hesitated. "I could bring my own tent."

"Do you have one?"

"No, but I'd have time to go into town and pick one up."

"That seems silly. Mine sleeps two."

Now there was an encouraging remark. He didn't think they'd spend the whole time sleeping but decided not to say so. "I'd be honored to be your Sherpa. I'm good at carrying things, setting up tents and building fires. I'd bring the food and do all the cooking. And I'll drive us there in my new truck." He was already picturing that it would be black.

"That makes no sense. The ranch is on the way to the refuge. If you come, I should just swing by and pick you up."

"That would be fine." He still needed to buy that truck, but maybe not tomorrow.

"I was planning to leave around four. The best times to film the horses are at dusk and dawn."

He thought about all the time that left in between but again decided to keep his mouth shut about it. Instead he offered her a way out of taking him along in case she had any second thoughts. "If I go along, I promise not to mess with your schedule for getting good videos. But if you'd rather go out there alone, I'll back off. I'd never want to interfere with your job."

She reached out and touched his cheek. "Don't back off. Persistence is sexy."

Capturing her hand, he turned his head so he could place a kiss in her palm.

She moaned softly and pulled her hand away. "And so are you. Let's go back before we both forget this is only our first date."

Chapter Five

Drew put the dirty dishes and anything food-related in the metal cooler while Austin smothered the fire. He told her the ice chest was fairly critter-proof and should be okay until he drove out with the ranch truck in a little while to haul everything back and make sure the fire was out.

"But we can take the blanket." He shook it out, folded it and handed it to her. "If you wouldn't mind holding it on the way back."

"Or I could sit on it. That might make more sense." She wasn't sure why he wanted to take the blanket when he was leaving the rest of the gear, but she'd go along with the plan.

"Actually, I want you to stuff it between us."

"You want me to… Oh, I get it." She managed not to laugh. "A barrier."

"The trip out here was painful, especially going over

bumps." He tugged on the brim of his hat. "Now that I've kissed you, the ride back will be even worse."

"I'm really glad I'm a girl."

He laughed. "Yes, ma'am, so am I. Let's go." He swung his leg over the ATV and sat down.

She climbed on after him and sandwiched the folded blanket between them. "I'll still need to hold on to you." She wrapped her arms around both the blanket and him. Not nearly as much fun as she'd had without the extra padding, but she didn't want to make the poor guy suffer.

"That's okay. I'm just trying to avoid having you pressed tight against my backside."

"What if I drove?"

"That would be worse."

She imagined his arms wrapped around her middle just below her breasts and her bottom nestled in the V of his legs. Her pulse kicked up a notch. "Guess so. Next time we do this you should probably just drive the truck out here and forget about the ATV."

"Next time we do this I don't plan to be in a constant state of arousal. Ready?"

"Y-yes." She managed to get the word out, but her brain had stalled on his last statement. She'd never met a person more goal-oriented than Austin.

She was beginning to understand what Cade meant. Being with Austin was a little like booking a ticket on a high-speed train and she could be in for a thrilling ride. She might regret allowing him to go along on this video trip because of all the ramifications, but she seriously doubted that he'd get in her way.

If anything, he might make things easier because he was more experienced at camping than she was. The more she thought about it, the more she looked forward to showing him something inspirational right here in

Wyoming. Those mustangs were descended from horses ridden by Spaniards looking for adventure two hundred years ago. That should appeal to him.

Mostly, though, she was excited about exploring a relationship with a man, both sexually and emotionally, without her family members knowing about it. They'd met and evaluated nearly everyone she'd dated except a few times when she'd only gone out with the guy once. Setting up this overnight camping trip with Austin seemed strange because he hadn't been vetted. But ultimately it felt liberating.

When they pulled up in front of the ranch house, she was very glad they hadn't continued to make out furiously on that blanket because Rosie and Herb sat on the front porch with a cowboy she didn't recognize.

Austin did, though. "Jonah, is that you? I thought you were driving over tomorrow!"

"Got off a day earlier so I just headed out." The cowboy ambled down the steps toward them.

"And why wouldn't you? We've gotta be more fun than the folks in Pinedale." Austin dismounted from the ATV and then helped her climb off.

"That's the truth, bro."

Drew left the blanket on the seat and turned to meet another returning foster son. His name sounded familiar but she'd heard so many recently that they were all blurring together.

Austin gestured toward the newcomer. "Drew Martinelli, I'd like you to meet Jonah Bridger, Zen master."

Jonah shook her hand. "Pleased to meet you, ma'am. Don't pay attention to that Zen stuff Austin's spouting. I'm not a master of anything. But Rosie and Herb tell me that you're the best videographer in Wyoming."

"That's stretching it, but it's nice to hear."

"Ah, she's just modest." Austin gave his foster brother a hug. "Like you are, bro. With all that meditating you used to do, you must be enlightened by now."

"'Fraid not. I've learned just enough to be dangerous."

"And to conduct Cade and Lexi's ceremony." Austin clapped him on the back. "I'm gonna get a kick out of that."

"Oh, right!" Drew remembered now. "You're the minister."

"With no church and no parishioners," Jonah said.

"So how does that work?" All Drew's relatives had been married in a church.

"I work at a dude ranch, and my boss wanted to offer weddings to our guests. He asked me if I'd be willing to get qualified to marry folks. You can apply online. It sounded like fun so I did it."

Austin nodded. "I can see how it would be fun being the person who launches a couple on their great adventure."

"Then you should get into it."

"Nope, not my thing. I have other plans in the hopper. But I look forward to seeing your performance on Saturday."

Drew realized that she'd heard Austin mention his future plans but he'd never been specific about them. She'd have to ask him about it tomorrow night. Right now, though, she needed to make her exit. These guys had some catching up to do, and at some point Austin had to drive back out to the clearing and gather the cookout gear.

She laid her hand on his arm. "Thanks for a great dinner. I'm going to head home." She glanced over at his brother. "Great to meet you, Jonah."

He touched the brim of his hat. "Same here, Drew."

She raised her voice. "Rosie and Herb, I'm going home. Have a good night."

"Come on up and sit for a while," Rosie called back. "Have some coffee."

"Thanks. I'll take a rain check." She turned back to Austin and smiled. "See you tomorrow afternoon."

"I'll walk you to your truck." He looked over at Jonah. "Be right back."

"Take your time."

She didn't bother to tell him that walking her to her truck, which was only a few yards away, was completely unnecessary. She suspected he'd want to open her door for her and give her a hand up. In truth, she was beginning to cherish that about him.

Once they'd reached the driver's side they had a small measure of privacy. She kept her voice low. "Are you sure you wouldn't rather stick around here tomorrow night and spend time with Jonah? You two seem fairly close."

"We lived in the same cabin once I was old enough to move out of the ranch house. He's a great guy and I'm glad he's here, but the answer is no, I wouldn't rather hang out here tomorrow. I want to be with you."

"All right." The intensity in his gaze made her heart race. "Then I'll see you at four."

He opened her door. "Don't bring any food. That'll be my contribution."

"Understood, but I'll ice up the chest so it's ready for the food. Having a chef along will be a treat."

He nudged back his hat and grinned. "Well, maybe food won't be my only contribution, come to think of it."

"Hey, don't go getting me hot and bothered."

"Do I?"

"You know you do."

"Good." He leaned down and gave her a quick kiss.

Then he helped her into the truck, closed the door and stepped back.

She had to get her keys from under the seat and when she looked out the window he was still there, feet braced apart, thumbs through his belt loops, looking amazing. She gave a little wave and he touched the brim of his hat.

Somehow she managed to start the engine and drive away even though her mind was completely occupied by the image of Austin standing in the driveway. She'd be sharing a small tent with that gorgeous cowboy within twenty-four hours and the concept left her breathless. It wasn't until she'd started down the dark ranch road that she realized she'd forgotten to turn on her headlights.

Austin climbed the steps to the porch where Jonah had resumed his seat next to Rosie. He and Herb each had a beer but his foster mom was sipping from a coffee mug that probably contained her favorite evening beverage, maybe her favorite beverage period—coffee laced with a little Baileys.

She lowered the mug to smile at him. "Did you have a good time?"

"We had a great time. Thank you for loaning me all that stuff. I'd better get back out there and pick it up, though. If I could borrow the ranch truck one more time, that should be it for a while."

Jonah put down his beer and stood. "We can take my truck. I wouldn't mind paying a visit to the back twenty."

"Hasn't changed much," Herb said. "Same scrub brush, same rocks around the perimeter."

"But it must be overgrown with weeds by now."

"It was a few months ago." Herb cradled his beer in both hands. "But this summer I started taking the academy kids out there for sleepovers. They've cleaned out the weeds."

"So that's why I didn't have much to do." Austin had raked a little but the place had looked as if it had been used regularly. Apparently the teens enrolled in the recently launched equine program would carry on some of the traditions the foster brothers had helped create.

"It's great to think of the kids enjoying the same things we did." Jonah walked over to join Austin before turning back to Rosie and Herb. "Listen, if you two want to hit the sack, you can leave my beer where it is. I'll come back to it after we finish up."

"We'll still be here," Rosie said. "Unless you boys dawdle."

"Then we'll see you soon." Austin walked with Jonah toward the barn where Jonah's beat-up truck was parked.

"Drew's pretty," Jonah said.

Austin chuckled. "That doesn't even begin to describe her."

"I know that, but I have to be careful. If I get too detailed, you might punch me."

"No, I wouldn't. I know you better than that. You don't poach."

"None of us ever did. I mean, think about it. I'll bet at one time or another all of us had a crush on Lexi. But once Cade made his move, that was it, hands off." He fished his keys out of his pocket. "I suppose you got the word that we're all considered part of the Thunder Mountain Brotherhood now."

"Cade told me. It's kind of nice, you know?"

"It is nice." Jonah climbed behind the wheel and Austin got into the passenger seat. Neither of them buckled up and they ignored the warning beeps as Jonah shoved the key into the ignition and turned it. "I won't lie. I was jealous of Cade, Damon and Finn."

"Yeah, most of us were."

"But imagine what it must have been like." Jonah put the truck in gear and drove past the front porch with a little friendly honk for Rosie and Herb. Then he headed down the narrow path to the campout clearing. "They were only thirteen. Hell, Finn was twelve. They didn't know there would be other foster boys eventually. No wonder they declared themselves blood brothers so they'd have something to hold on to. I can see how they'd be proud and protective of that status."

"I can, too." Austin settled back in the seat. "I decided to say thanks for including us instead of being a jerk about it."

"Same here. You know, I've missed this place."

"So have I, which is why I'm back."

"I'm thinking about it, too. Mom asked me if I'd like the caretaking job over at Matt's ranch. I'm considering it, but there are drawbacks."

"Yep. Nothing's really yours."

"I could handle that. Possessions aren't a big deal to me. But when Matt comes home and brings his fiancée, I'll feel like the butler."

Austin laughed. "How's your English accent?"

"Lousy. What he needs is a caretaker's cabin. Doesn't have to be fancy. I'd help put it up. If he'll agree to that, then I'll give my notice and move back here."

"And leave your dude ranch without a preacher man?"

"I'll make sure that's worked out before I leave." He glanced over at Austin. "Not to change the subject, but I'm changing the subject. I'm curious about Drew."

"What about her?"

"Mom and Dad said you've been home for all of two

days. I'll admit those muscles you acquired in New Zealand are impressive, but damn, that's fast work, even for someone as focused as you."

"I don't know what to tell you. This afternoon I was under the sink getting rid of a clog. Cade and Lexi came into the kitchen to grab a beer and then the videographer walked in. I scooted out from under the sink and saw my future."

"Your *future*? That sounds like something out of a movie. But then, you've been a dreamer ever since I've known you. The problem is, life doesn't work that way."

"Of course it doesn't if you just let the chips fall. I didn't get to New Zealand by hoping that some magical event would take me there. I worked my ass off, saved my money and made it happen."

"True, but—"

"Drew is no different. Maybe she's not the right one for me, but I have a gut feeling she is. I didn't expect to find her two days after I landed in Wyoming, but what if that's my reward for making the decision to move back and look for a wife?"

"Oh, jeez. You've known her since sometime this afternoon and you already think you'll end up marrying her? What's wrong with you?"

"I know it sounds crazy."

"Yes, it absolutely does. I'm thinking the water in New Zealand has altered your brain chemistry."

"There's nothing wrong with my brain chemistry."

Jonah sighed. "You're not a competent judge of that. When we get back to the house, we're going to have some beers while I convince you to slow down and take stock. Oh, and whatever you do, don't have sex with her. It's impossible to think clearly when you're doing the horizontal mambo with someone. Which reminds me, what was the deal with that blanket wedged between you two on the ATV?"

"We were just goofing around." Austin smiled and decided not to mention the plan for tomorrow night.

Chapter Six

Underwear. Drew stared into her dresser drawer, having a stupid debate with herself. She had some silky panties and bras but they weren't as comfortable as cotton for hiking. They didn't breathe.

But her breathable cotton was white and made her look like a jock. Which she was. Except with the guys she'd dated in Billings, she'd tried to present a different image. That was why she had silk and lace undies in black, red and purple. Maybe that was the reason she hadn't clicked with any of those men. She'd been trying to be someone different.

She glanced at the clock on her bedroom wall. The truck was loaded. She'd showered and shaved her legs with a new razor. All she had to do was get dressed and throw a change of clothes in a duffel and she'd be good to go.

Finally, she grabbed two pairs of cotton panties and two cotton sports bras, one set to put on now and the other to toss in the duffel. She didn't know why she'd spent so much time thinking about it. This was who she was. In fact, she should get rid of the others, bag them up and donate them to charity.

If Austin had a negative reaction to her utilitarian underwear he wasn't someone she cared to spend time with. That would be good to know before they had sex.

When she left her apartment and got into her truck, she had her hair in a ponytail that was pulled through a forest green Rocky Mountain College baseball cap. She'd tucked her tan long-sleeved shirt into some old jeans that allowed her to move easily. She wore her necklace under her shirt with the pendant inside her bra.

Heavy socks and a sturdy pair of hiking boots finished off an outfit that wasn't the least bit glamorous. She hadn't talked to him about footwear. Maybe she should have.

She drove over to the ranch to get Austin. When he walked out to meet her carrying a duffel and a couple of bags from the grocery store, he looked amazing as always in a yoked shirt, brown Stetson and jeans that fit him like a glove. But he was wearing cowboy boots. She should have warned him not to.

She managed to get out of the truck before he came around to open the door. His chivalry was fun and all, but it could slow them down and she didn't want to waste any time getting out to the refuge. "Do you have any hiking boots to wear instead?"

"Not really."

"You didn't hike in New Zealand?"

"No, ma'am. The idea was to ride the trail, not hike it."

"Sorry. We should have talked about this. We'll be parking next to the road and then hiking in to set up camp. It's more than a mile. To film the horses, we'll have to hike some more. Do you have anything else? Running shoes?"

"I have an old grungy pair, but I hate to—"

"You should go put those on while I load the food in the ice chest." She could tell he didn't like the idea. "Really, I'm serious. We could end up hiking a couple of miles to find the horses, maybe more. You'll be miserable in those boots."

"All right." He handed her the bags of food and his duffel. "Be right back."

She let down the tailgate, crawled into the truck bed and loaded the ice chest with the food he'd brought. The supplies included another bottle of the wine they'd had the night before. She had to admit having a guy provide a gourmet meal in a campground setting was arousing in its own way.

She'd finished stashing the food and had closed the tailgate when he came back down the steps in a pair of running shoes that might have been white once but were now a sad-looking gray. They weren't snazzy like his boots but they'd serve him better.

"I'm glad you have those," she said as he approached.

"It's a wonder I still do. They're close to ten years old. I bought them so I could run track in high school."

"Why would a cowboy who doesn't hike want to run track?"

"There was this girl on the team, and I—"

"Okay, never mind." Then she had another thought. "Are you pretending to be interested in these horses? Because I think they're super cool but if you're only going along because of the tent-sharing possibility, then we should rethink this."

He met her gaze. "The tent-sharing element is a huge draw. But I also want to see the mustangs. Before I went to bed last night I used Mom's computer and looked up their history. Exciting stuff."

"Isn't it?" She was pleased that he'd taken the time to research. "They've survived against all odds and that says something about their resilience."

"I'm all about resilience."

Considering his background, he'd have to be. "Then let's go find some Pryor Mountain mustangs." She walked around to the driver's side.

"You bet." He followed her.

Although his insistence on gentlemanly behavior made her want to giggle, she accepted his help getting in. "Thank you."

"My pleasure." He touched the brim of his hat with the tips of his fingers before jogging around the front of the truck and climbing in. "Let's go."

She started the engine and pulled away from the ranch house. "I have a hypothetical question."

"Shoot."

"Let's say that we're being chased by a bear while we're out on the trail and we manage to reach the truck."

"First of all, never try to outrun a bear."

"I actually know that. All right, something else is chasing us. A cougar."

"Can't outrun them, either. And they're really shy so chances are you won't see one, let alone be chased."

"Pretend it's a female who thinks we're threatening her kittens. And she's a little slow. We've managed to reach the truck. Are you with me so far?"

He grinned at her. "I can't wait to see how this turns out."

"How would you handle things at that point?"

"Simple. I'd distract the cougar while you got in the truck."

She was glad to hear he wouldn't insist on opening her door first. "But that's not logical. If we split up and I head for the driver's side and you head for the passenger side, we both have a good chance of reaching safety before the cougar attacks."

"Or the cougar could decide to follow you and I'd be safe and you'd be toast. I'm not taking that chance."

He said it with such certainty that she had no doubt he would react that way. "You'd risk your life for someone you barely know?"

"I'd argue the term *barely know*, but yes, I would. My dad had never met that family he rescued."

"And he made an incredibly selfless sacrifice. Most people wouldn't have. But he was also a trained professional dedicated to that job. We're just out on a camping trip together. You're not responsible for my safety." From the corner of her eye she could see he was smiling. "What?"

"I could ask where this is coming from, but I think I know since your hypothetical question popped up right after I helped you into your truck. You've never dated a cowboy before, have you?"

"No."

"Then maybe I should explain how we operate. We open doors for ladies. We hold their chairs and help them on with their coats. That's surface stuff, but we'll also fight off the cougar if it becomes necessary." He glanced at her and shrugged. "It's what we do."

"That's—"

"Old-fashioned, I know. And you're an independent woman who can open her own door and wants to give the guy you're with a chance to outrun the cougar. I get that."

"I was going to say, 'that's nice.'"

"Yeah?"

"Yeah. I am an independent woman, at least that's my goal, and obviously I can open my own door. I'd feel horrible if I got away from the cougar and you didn't. But knowing you are willing to throw yourself into the breach on my account is nice. More than nice. If that's how cowboys operate, I'm a fan."

"Excellent news." He settled back with a sigh. "I see you left your pendant at home."

"No, I didn't."

"Where is it?"

"Under my shirt. That works better for hiking and filming."

He nodded. "Makes sense."

After that they rode in companionable silence until they reached the outskirts of town. Well, maybe *companionable silence* wasn't the right description because that implied a relaxed mood. Perhaps *alert silence* was more accurate, at least on her part. Once they stopped talking she became aware of how much space he occupied, both emotionally and physically.

She'd had other guys in her passenger seat before but Austin affected her in ways no one else did. He had presence. Maybe it was the strong profile and the Stetson, or the broad shoulders and the massive chest. It could be his aftershave, which reminded her that he knew how to kiss. She wanted to keep looking at him, although she didn't or they'd be in a ditch by now.

His thigh was within touching distance and so was his muscled biceps. She longed to reach over and— Nope, not going there. She'd do well to come up with another topic of conversation before she embarrassed herself.

Driving through town on the way to the interstate reminded her that he'd planned to buy a truck. That should be a safe topic. "Did you go vehicle shopping today?"

"No, ma'am. Decided to go tomorrow, instead. Jonah and I helped Lexi string minilights in the rafters of the barn."

"That will be beautiful for the ceremony. I can't wait to see how the lights look when we do the run-through on Friday night."

"And that will only give you part of the effect. The flowers won't go in until Saturday, although Cade realized the wall vases and velvet bows have to be out of reach of the horses or they'll eat them."

Drew laughed and felt her sexual tension ease somewhat. "I'm sure Cade and Lexi would hate that but it would make a funny video."

"Speaking of videos, Lexi said she loves the one you did of her and Cade."

"I know she does and that thrills me. She sent me a glowing email. Honestly, I would have had to work hard to make a bad video of those two. They're so relaxed with each other and so in love. I guess that's what comes from knowing someone for half your life."

"Then there are couples like Rosie and Herb. Rosie moved here from Illinois to take a job in social services. They met in the checkout line at the grocery store. A month later they were married."

"I'll bet that's unusual, though."

"Maybe. But my parents had only known each other for about six months. My mom said my dad was the love of her life."

Drew glanced over and he was staring out the window. "They sound like terrific people, Austin. I wish they hadn't been taken away from you."

"So do I." He turned back to her and his expression was calm. "But Rosie and Herb are terrific people, too. I'm a lucky guy."

"When you put it like that, yes, you are. And you have a wonderful home to come back to. By the way, you said something to Jonah last night about your future plans. Have you already applied for a job somewhere?"

"I haven't yet, but if I can swing it, I want to go into business for myself. I paid close attention to how the New Zealand outfit ran things and I figure I can handle something similar over here."

"Of course you can!" This was a topic she could dig into. "And I'm here to tell you that self-employment is a great way to go."

"Any advice on creating a website?"

"Sure. I can help you with that." She loved the idea of someone starting a business and Austin seemed like the perfect person to do it. He was personable and had four years of valuable experience to guide him. But his real gift was the focus he would bring to the project.

As they exited the interstate onto the two-lane road that would take them into Bighorn Canyon, Austin described his plans for trailering horses into the canyon for two- and three-day trail rides.

"That sounds fabulous. If you want, I could go along on one of the first rides and shoot video you could use for the website."

"Great idea. I'd pay, you of course."

"Or how about this? Only snippets will go on the website, but I could offer to sell the full video to your trail riders. I'm sure they'd buy it as a souvenir. Then you wouldn't have to come out of pocket."

"Brilliant strategy. Thank you. Now I wish it was May instead of August. There's no way I can get this up and running before winter weather hits."

"But you can use the coming months to put everything in place so you're ready by next May."

"And arrange for a business loan. I should probably apply for a bartending job at Scruffy's for the winter months, too. When I was saving for New Zealand I worked as a waiter until I was old enough to bartend. That gig was way better money. The tips were awesome."

"I'll bet." A bartender who looked like Austin would get tipped well by any women who stopped by Scruffy's. "It's smart of you to launch your business here in Sheridan, where you know so many people. Being connected to Rosie and Herb will give you a huge PR boost."

"I never considered doing it anywhere else. This is home. I'm here to stay."

"Wouldn't you like to travel some more?"

"Maybe someday. For now, I have things to do here and I plan to concentrate on that."

"Well, if there's any way I can help, just let me know. I'm no expert, but I've learned a little about promotion. Then there's bookkeeping and taxes to think about and I can offer some suggestions there."

"Excellent. I appreciate it. I want this to work."

"I'm sure it will." She was surprised that he wasn't including more travel in his immediate vision of the future after experiencing a wonderful place like New Zealand. But maybe that was the secret to his success. He set himself a goal and refused to be distracted until he'd achieved it.

Which reminded her that she hadn't clearly identified long-term goals for herself. When her grandmother had given her the necklace, she'd also given her three words of advice—*Follow your heart*. Drew had hoped getting away from her family would help her do that, but so far she was still living one day at a time.

"I just saw a couple of mule deer scamper up that hillside." Austin peered out the side window. "No cougars, though. Sorry."

"Yeah, yeah, yeah. I know that was a lame example. I've never seen one out here, but I know they're around. Others have reported sightings."

"Just don't run."

"Oh, I won't. Because then you'll end up being mauled and it'll be my fault." She watched for the rock outcroppings that she used as a marker. "We'll be stopping in another mile or so. I get so excited when one of the herds is spotted within a couple of miles of my favorite camping spot. The folks who are monitoring them emailed me today. The horses are still there."

"How often do you make this trip?"

"This is my third time in this particular area but I've camped in other places, so I guess it's seven visits, total. I don't always get good footage. Depends on the horses and the weather. But it's supposed to stay clear through tomorrow."

"I have a feeling this will be a good outing."

She gave him a quick smile. "Hope so." She slowed down and eased the truck to the right shoulder of the road. "We'll take the tent in first and set that up to claim our campsite. I usually haul my duffel along and leave that in the tent, too. Nobody will bother it."

"That works for me." He unbuckled his seat belt and opened the door.

"Austin." She laid a hand on his arm.

"What?"

"I love your cowboy manners, but don't come around and open my door for me. We're close to the road and there's no reason for both of us to be over there."

He let out a breath. "When you're right, you're right. But be careful."

"I will. I'll meet you out there. Go ahead and pull the tent out if you want." She let a truck go by before quickly getting out and walking back to him.

Instead of lowering the tailgate and getting the tent as she'd suggested, he stood by the back bumper and watched her approach as if his vigilance would prevent her from getting run over. He was so manly, so strong and sure of himself that she almost believed he could protect her by keeping her in view.

As her gaze locked with his, she felt a magnetic, sensual tug. She wanted this man and he most definitely wanted her. For one brief moment she considered abandoning her plan to film the mustangs. Her breath caught. That she'd even think such a thing was a wake-up call.

She'd enthusiastically leaped to support his dreams yet she hadn't solidified her own. She needed to be careful.

Chapter Seven

Austin nominated himself to lug the tent, two blankets and a couple of self-inflating camping mattresses to the campsite. Drew wore her backpack full of camera equipment and carried both duffels as she led the way. As he followed her along a faint path, he kept thinking they'd be there any minute but she'd told him the truth about hiking in a ways.

Bringing the food in later would mean another long walk out to the road and back, but at least they wouldn't be able to hear traffic during the night. So far he'd loved every minute of this trip—minus the dorky shoes—and he knew why. For the first time he was beginning a relationship that had the potential to become so much more.

Prior to leaving for New Zealand, he'd never felt right making long-term promises to women because he'd known he would leave. Dating in New Zealand had been the same story—no commitment. That wasn't his style. He craved meaning in his life and especially in his love life.

Drew had worn the pendant from her grandmother again today and he took that loyalty as a good sign. He could never get serious about a woman who didn't care deeply. Drew obviously did.

"Here we are!" She dropped both duffels and took off her backpack as they stood in a little grassy clearing ringed with tall pines. A scattering of wildflowers, including some yellow daisies and purple lupines, gave the area a nice splash of color. Charred pieces of firewood in a small, stone-lined pit indicated that others had been here. She pointed to it. "I built that and I dragged the log out of the forest so there's a place to sit."

"Nice job." He lowered the tent and the mattresses to the ground and put the blankets on top.

"We should probably collect some firewood before we head off to find the horses. Sometimes I've skipped doing that and FYI, it's not easy to find kindling in a dark forest."

"That used to be one of our mantras in New Zealand. *Firewood before food.*"

"We don't need it for dinner, though. Like I mentioned last night, I have a camp stove. But I like a fire to signal other campers that we're here."

"Then we need to get busy." He eyed the long nylon bag containing the tent. It was an older dome model and he remembered struggling with the bendable supports when he'd had one years ago. "I'll bet you've had some fun times setting the tent up by yourself."

She laughed. "I have, but I'm used to it by now." She walked over and loosened the nylon cord holding the top of the bag. "If you want to go look for firewood, I'll set it up."

He wasn't about to go off and leave her to do it alone. He'd promised to be an asset and despite what she'd said about being used to the process, it would go faster with two people. "I'll help."

"Okay, but I have to warn you. This tent has a unique personality. She responds better to coaxing than yelling."

"*She*? Your tent has a gender?"

"Of course. Doesn't yours?"

"I sold mine before I left New Zealand but I never considered it male or female."

"Which means you didn't name it, either."

He stuck his thumbs in his belt loops. "Can't say as I did, but I like the idea. Now I wish I had. Are you telling me this tent has a name?"

"She does. Meet Hestia, the Greek goddess of the hearth."

"I like it. Hestia, I look forward to spending time with you."

"Now, see? That's exactly the right attitude." Drew pulled a blue tent out of the bag. "This will go just fine."

A minute into the job, he was cursing under his breath as he wrestled with the plastic supports. He had to be careful because if he broke one, they'd have a mess. "Hestia's not cooperating."

"I hear you cussing over there. You need to speak nicely to her." Drew began murmuring sweet nothings to the tent, and damned if they didn't get the thing set up a lot quicker.

They worked together to unroll the mattresses and spread out the blankets. Neither of them spoke and he wondered if she was thinking what he was. They were making the bed they were planning to share.

At last they were done. He stood and brushed off his knees. She did the same. They had created a temporary home that would shelter them during the night and provide a place for…he glanced over at Drew and she was looking right back at him. The air between them seemed to vibrate.

Taking a deep breath, she broke eye contact. "You can put our duffels inside and zip it up tight. I need to go back to the truck. I meant to bring my little first aid kit and I left it in the console."

"I can get it."

"That's okay. I will. How about collecting the firewood while I'm gone? I'll bring the hatchet from the truck. Might as well have everything here except the food." The message in her dark eyes was clear. *Let's take a break.*

He doubted she needed that first aid kit but if she went after it she could spend the time cooling down. He'd use the separation to do the same. "I'll see what I can find. Meet you back here."

Turning away from her, he walked toward the tree line. He'd promised her that he wouldn't interfere with her primary mission, to get video of the Pryor Mountain horses. If he screwed that up, then he'd ruin any chance they had of transforming this attraction into something special.

Years ago, he'd learned the value of foregoing short-term gain for long-term reward. He wanted to kiss her in the worst way, had wanted to ever since she'd pulled into the driveway at Thunder Mountain. He'd successfully controlled the urge. He didn't want her to think that all he cared about was getting physical.

That wasn't true. She was easy to talk to and the drive out here had been fun, although he'd spent some time thinking about what they'd likely be doing tonight. Now that they had a tent and a bed, the concept was more vivid than ever. But the mustangs had to be first on the list.

After loading up his arms with small branches, he found a big one and dragged that behind him as he returned to camp. She wasn't back yet but he hadn't expected her to be. Gathering wood hadn't taken long.

Putting the duffels in the tent wouldn't, either, but he did that next and zipped it closed. Too bad he didn't have that hatchet yet. He could work off some tension chopping wood.

When he saw her coming down the trail toward him, his pulse kicked into high gear. Everything about her appealed to him. He liked the graceful way she moved and the mellow tone of her voice. He liked her laughter and her easy way with others. He liked the way she looked in her Rocky Mountain College baseball cap.

She gave him a smile as she approached and he returned it. He thought about walking to meet her but changed his mind and stayed where he was. For the next few hours, he would take his cues from her.

"I see you got the firewood. That big piece should last us a week."

"I'll chop it up for the next campers. That's an interesting combination, a hatchet in one hand and a first aid kit in the other."

"I'm hoping we only have to make use of the hatchet." She put it near the pile of kindling he'd gathered. "I'll take this with us, though." Walking over to her backpack, she unzipped a pocket and tucked the first aid kit inside. "For one thing, it has bug bite cream." She picked up the backpack by its straps.

"Why not let me carry that?"

She paused to glance at him. "I guess you did say you'd be my Sherpa. Okay, thanks." She took a small camcorder out of the front section. "I want to leave this out for quick shots, in case we come upon something unexpectedly."

"Like a cougar."

"Like that." She grinned. "All joking aside, getting footage of a cougar would be awesome. But they're so elusive that chances are slim."

"I've never seen one, either, and I've lived here most of my life." He slipped the straps over his shoulders and adjusted them. "Ready?"

She nodded. "The trail's over this way." She gestured toward a break in the trees. "It's faint and disappears when we go over rocks, so don't lag behind. I'll be concentrating on what's ahead of us and if you stop to look at something I could be out of sight before you realize it."

"I plan to stick like glue." He matched her brisk pace as they crossed the clearing.

"And let's keep talking to a minimum. The more noise we make, the less wildlife we'll see."

"Understood." He fell in behind her on the narrow trail and focused on keeping her in sight. It wasn't a chore. He enjoyed watching her confident strides as they walked along the path.

Speaking of walking, or *hiking*, a word that made it sound more like a manly sport, he concluded it wasn't his thing. There were reasons cowboys didn't hike and he was discovering them all today.

The mountain air smelled piney and fresh like he was used to, but there was something missing. He finally figured out it was the scent of oiled leather and horse sweat. He heard birds twittering like normal, but there was no clop, clop of hooves and the occasional snorting and blowing.

Another thing about this hiking business—it was slow as molasses. It took them forever to wind through the forest, cross a meadow, pick up the trail on the other side and work their way through the trees again. A horse could have made it in less than half the time.

Besides, the view from the ground was terrible compared to the vista he was used to. Elevated by a horse about sixteen hands high, he'd have a much better idea where they were headed and probably catch a breeze easier, too.

He adjusted the straps on the backpack again. It wasn't that heavy, but it was cumbersome. If he had a horse, the equipment could be strapped behind the saddle or tucked into saddlebags.

He suspected trail rides weren't allowed in the refuge, though. Bringing domesticated horses in contact with wild ones might not be a great idea. That didn't keep him from longing for a sturdy mount and his totally broken-in saddle. He'd shipped it over to New Zealand and shipped it back. It was just that important.

But he'd gotten himself into this situation because of the fine-looking woman walking ahead of him, her glossy dark ponytail bobbing with each step. He didn't regret asking to go along on this trip considering he had a good chance of seeing wild horses and spending quality time with Drew.

But he could say with complete assurance that he was not, and probably never would be, a hiker. She was, though. Maybe if he had boots like hers, with all that tread—nah, wouldn't help. He'd still be walking instead of riding.

His mom used to say she felt a little closer to heaven on the back of a horse. So did he. A little closer to her, too, now that he thought about it. He couldn't remember his first ride because she'd held him in front of her before he was a year old. He had pictures to prove it.

A soft flapping noise and the way his shoe was slipping made him glance down. Great. One of his shoelaces had come untied. He was out of practice wearing running shoes and he'd forgotten to tie an extra knot.

That was one of the things he loved about cowboy boots—no laces. They always looked good, too. Even old scuffed ones did because they had character. Old running shoes just looked nasty.

He dropped to one knee and called out to Drew. "Hang on a sec. I need to tie my—"

"Shh." She stopped walking but didn't turn around. "I hear them. And they're close."

He stopped tying his shoe to listen. If he'd been paying attention he would have heard them, too. His breath caught when he spotted dark shapes walking through the trees, pine needles crunching and branches cracking under their hooves. He estimated the mustangs were only about thirty feet ahead of them and closing.

"We need to move away," Drew said in a low voice as she edged off the trail and to the right. But she had her camcorder pointed at the dark shapes threading their way through the forest on their left. "We're supposed to maintain a one-hundred-foot distance."

"Did anybody tell them that?" But he backed off, too, all the while keeping an eye on his dangling shoelace. If he tripped and went down, all hell would break loose. Even trained horses might bolt at a sudden loud crash.

The dappled shade made it tough to identify color but he thought they were mostly bays. Maybe a buckskin or two. There was a gray bringing up the rear. He counted ten but might have missed some. His heart hammered. He'd been around horses all his life but he'd never seen a wild one.

These animals had never felt the weight of a saddle,

let alone the weight of a person. Instead of human rules, they obeyed the rules of the herd in exchange for protection and companionship. They ate what they could forage. They mated and gave birth with no interference from humans.

Seeing them in their natural state affected him on a gut level that likely would make a difference in the way he thought about horses for the rest of his life. Now that he'd had his first glimpse, he'd be back and he'd have on good hiking boots. If he'd been riding instead of walking, the experience might never have happened. Even if it had, it wouldn't have been nearly this elemental. Maybe hiking wasn't so bad, after all.

Drew didn't switch off her camcorder until the gray horse bringing up the rear was out of sight. "They might be headed toward the meadow we just left." Her voice trembled with excitement. "At first I thought I recognized some of them, but now I think this is a band I haven't filmed yet, which is awesome. We might catch them grazing if we backtrack."

"Let's do it. Just have to tie my shoelace." He quickly made a double knot and did the same with the other one. "Okay. Go."

Instead of immediately taking off down the trail, she paused to gaze up at him, her dark eyes gleaming with anticipation. "Cool, huh?"

"*Very* cool. I wouldn't have missed it for the world. Thank you."

"I was hoping you'd love them."

"I do. They're amazing."

"I know." With a quick smile, she turned and started off, her ponytail swinging.

As he followed her, the warm emotion gripping him had a little to do with sexual attraction but a lot more to do with friendship. He and Drew were bonding over their shared appreciation for these mustangs. He let out a slow breath. At last he had the freedom to connect with a woman without thinking he was liable to mess up her life.

Chapter Eight

Because the lighting had been funky when Drew had tried to get footage of the horses moving through the trees, she didn't think she had much of value. But if the herd stopped to graze in the meadow she and Austin had just hiked across, she might get lucky.

Adrenaline pumped through her system, partly because these weren't the horses she'd been expecting. Filming old friends was great, but having a chance to get shots of a different band would be more exciting. Assuming she got some worth looking at, she'd show them to the experts at the Pryor Mountain center in Lovell. Those folks had named and could identify nearly every mustang in the area.

She was also sharing Austin's high following his first encounter. She hadn't realized this trip was a litmus test. She couldn't be friends, let alone lovers, with someone who didn't respect and admire these wild mustangs, which symbolized freedom to her. His dazzled expression had told her all she needed to know.

When they were within ten yards of the meadow, she paused, turned around and motioned him closer. "I need to unload my tripod and my larger camera before we leave the cover of the trees," she murmured. "If they're out there, the less we move and make noise, the better. The breeze is blowing in our direction, which helps."

He eased the pack from his shoulders. "Take what you need."

Maybe if he hadn't said it so softly she wouldn't have had a sudden, vivid image of those words uttered in a different context and a different place, like in their shared tent. Heat scorched her body and she knew her cheeks must be red. "Thanks."

She kept her head down as she slowly unzipped the backpack. The rasp of the zipper took on erotic meaning in the X-rated movie playing in her head. Wrapping her hand around the tripod did, too.

Good grief, why did she have to be blindsided by lust *now*? She'd made it through the drive here and the tent setup, although she'd had to walk off some tension after that activity. Yes, the thrill of seeing the horses moving through the trees so close to them had stirred her blood.

But she'd fought and won the battle with her libido, which had urged her to kiss him afterward. Why had her mind betrayed her during this critical moment when she needed to focus?

He leaned down so his mouth was close to her ear. "Are you okay?"

His warm breath sent her pulse skyrocketing and she gulped for air. "Sure. Why?"

"You're panting."

More warm breath tickled her earlobe, which she'd never realized was an erogenous zone. "Just excited."

"I get that, but you're shaking, too. Did you eat today?"

"Yes." She pulled her tripod out of the backpack and nearly dropped it on his foot. She fumbled it like a football and eventually he gently took it from her.

He lowered the backpack to the ground and laid the tripod on top. "Let's go where we can talk." Taking her by the hand, he led her back down the path.

Every step of the way she wondered what in the world she could say to him that wouldn't make things worse.

When they were a few yards away from where they'd been standing, he grasped her shoulders and gave her a searching glance. "Something's wrong. I don't know if it's low blood sugar or what, but you're *not* okay. Whatever it is, I want to help."

She managed to hold back a bubble of hysterical laughter.

"You're turning red as a lobster. Don't be embarrassed. Just tell me." His grip tightened. "Do you need medication of some kind? Is that why you went back for the first aid kit? Are you allergic to something out here?"

She took a shaky breath. "It's you."

"Me?" He let go of her and stepped back, frowning. "Is it my aftershave? That can't be right because it's the same one I had on last night."

"It's stupid, but suddenly all I can think about is… kissing…you." She was thinking of way more than that but she'd decided against a full reveal.

Slowly his frown disappeared and he began to smile. "I don't call that stupid."

"Yes, it is. The horses are probably out there in the meadow, posing for their close-up, and I'm fantasizing about having sex with you." She clapped a hand over her mouth.

His smile widened. "More than kissing, then."

"I don't want to talk about it. That won't help and I *really* want to get some good video of those mustangs."

Hooking his thumbs in his belt loops, he took a long, slow breath before gazing at her, all teasing gone from his expression. "I want you to get that footage, too. If my being here ruins it for you, that's not good."

"It's not your fault." The concern in his eyes helped settle her down. He didn't want to be a distraction, and that counted for a lot. "Let's try it again, only I'll be in charge of the backpack and the equipment from now on. That should work better."

"Maybe I should cut through the trees and pick up the trail on the other side of the meadow. I'm sure I can find it and then I'll be out of your way."

"But you want to see the horses, too."

"I'll gladly give that up if I can solve your problem by leaving."

"I don't want you to leave. Maybe admitting my issues was half the battle because I'm calmer now. But FYI, if you need to communicate quietly, don't murmur in my ear. Apparently, that gets me hot."

His mouth twitched as if he wanted to smile but was working hard not to. "What should I do, then?"

"Touch me on the shoulder and mouth the words. I'm pretty good at reading lips."

He ducked his head and cleared his throat. "Got it."

"I don't blame you for wanting to laugh. It's pretty funny."

"Yes, ma'am." He looked up. "But in a good way. Ready to go?"

"Yes. I'll lead."

"Yes, ma'am."

She walked briskly toward her backpack and took out what she needed before closing it up and sliding the straps over her shoulders. Once she'd adjusted them, the familiar weight of the pack helped her feel more in charge. She glanced at Austin. "Let's see if they waited for us."

He smiled and mouthed *okay*.

At the edge of the trees, she eased out into the open and sucked in a quick breath. The mustangs were peacefully grazing about forty yards away a little to her right. The light was perfect, bringing out the gem-like green of the pines to form a nice background, especially for the gray horse. The breeze blowing toward her carried her scent away while delicately ruffling a mane here, a tail there. She was in video heaven.

Mounting her camcorder with as little noise as possible, she crouched down and panned slowly across the herd. The gray stopped eating, lifted its head and surveyed the meadow. She identified him as the stallion and that was confirmed as he began to circle the herd. He'd seen her.

Slowly she picked up her tripod and backed toward the trees. She'd become the uninvited guest at the dinner hour. They deserved to eat in peace.

She'd barely stepped into the shade when Austin tapped her on the shoulder. She turned and he pointed to her right, at the edge of the meadow. She'd been so focused on the horses and so certain that she was the harmless intruder that she'd missed the threatening one.

Creeping toward the herd, using low bushes as temporary cover and the breeze to hide its scent, was a cougar. Drew quickly removed the tripod and trained her camera on the cat. Excitement over her first sighting vied with dread for the horses, especially the small buckskin that seemed to be the cougar's target. As an observer of nature and a friend to all creatures, she couldn't intervene. The cougar had to eat and the mustang was prey.

Restlessly circling the herd, the stallion obviously sensed danger but couldn't identify the source. Then the breeze shifted. The stallion's nostrils flared and he trumpeted a warning. The cat leaped and missed the buckskin. Before the cougar could gather itself to try again, the herd took off at a dead run, their thundering hooves making the ground shake as they crashed through the trees on the far side of the meadow.

Drew recorded their flight. After they were gone, she panned the area for any sign of the cat and found nothing. Not surprising.

Austin stood next to her, gazing out at the empty meadow. "I've never seen anything like that."

"Quite a drama." She glanced over at him. "Which one did you root for?"

"The animal most determined to succeed."

How like him to answer that way. She really was starting to know who he was. "I'm not sure which one qualifies. The cougar had it won and then the breeze shifted."

"Yes, ma'am, but that stallion was on his game. He might not have smelled that cat but he knew something wasn't right."

"Because I was out there."

"I don't think you were an issue. I was watching him and he wasn't paying much attention to you. Some animals seem to know when they're in a protected area. He might not have let you walk right up to him, but I don't think humans worry him."

"I thought my being there was why he started circling the herd."

Austin shook his head. "Maybe, but that's not how I

saw it. The cougar showed up right after you went out there. As it started stalking the herd, the little birds that had been flitting around in the bushes got quiet and then they flew away."

"I didn't notice that."

"I'll bet the stallion did. He gets my vote as the most focused. The cat lost its advantage by being too cautious in the approach and waiting too long to spring."

She couldn't help smiling at that. "Is there a slight chance you identified with the stallion?"

"Yes, ma'am." He flashed her a charming, Austin-style grin. "Every cowboy identifies with stallions." He paused. "So what next? Want to track them? Shouldn't be too hard with the way they tore out of here."

She glanced up at the sky. "We're losing light."

"That's a fact."

"And when I was packing the food I noticed you brought another bottle of the New Zealand wine."

"That's another fact. Are you saying you'd like to go back to the campsite and settle in?"

"I'm saying exactly that. But, Austin…"

"What, pretty lady?"

"About the way I reacted a little while ago? I don't want you to get the idea that I'm some desperate—"

"Whoa, whoa. I don't see desperate. I see sensual and giving."

"Thank you. I like that description." She unzipped her backpack. "Let's get going. We need to haul in our food before it gets dark."

His gaze was warm. "Looks like it'll be a pleasure camping with you, ma'am."

"Ditto, Austin." She liked the way they could talk things out. Her small meltdown in the forest could have become a big deal if he hadn't gently put her back on course.

After she'd loaded her equipment into the backpack, he offered to carry it and promised not to murmur in her ear. Smiling, she turned over the pack. She didn't need to be in charge of the expedition anymore.

She had some video gems, though. She wouldn't use battery life to review what she'd taken but no question she'd struck gold. Although her meltdown had caused a minor delay, she'd been on hand to film a cougar's failed attempt to kill a mustang.

If she'd appeared in the meadow ten minutes earlier, everything could have been different. She'd worried about Austin being a distraction. He was, but she couldn't fault him for it any more than she could fault him for being gorgeous. He also might be her good luck charm, someone who helped make things happen.

The hike back took less time than the hike out because she wasn't looking for filming opportunities. Once they arrived, Austin stowed her pack in the tent and they started down the path to the road. The exercise during the day had left her so hungry her stomach was growling.

After all her solo camping, she had to admit having a strong guy around to carry things was nice. He lifted the ice chest out of the truck as if it weighed nothing. Then he set the camp stove and the lantern on top and said he could take it all.

Without help, she usually ended up making two trips to carry the camping gear and another two for the food and cookware. Having Austin along meant they'd brought more stuff, but it also meant fewer trips. She reached into the truck bed for a canvas drawstring bag of nonperishables and another one with her cookware and dishes.

Neither weighed much so she also grabbed the plastic

trash bag she'd stashed a couple of pillows in. She always brought one when she was camping. Camping mattresses worked okay but she hadn't met an inflatable pillow yet that suited her.

"What's the plan for after dinner?" He asked it so innocently that it didn't seem like a leading question.

But she was holding some of their bedding so she wasn't sure. She glanced over her shoulder. "You'll have to be more specific."

His blue eyes darkened. "I do believe you've tuned into the sexy channel again."

"Maybe." She left the bags on the tailgate and turned to face him. "Have you?"

"I have now." He put everything down before walking over to her. "But as it happens, I was asking how we'll keep critters from getting into our food supplies tonight while we're...asleep."

When she saw the heat in his eyes, she grew short of breath. "I have a thermal bag and a rope tucked in with the nonperishables. We'll store any food that will spoil in that and suspend all the bags from a tree branch."

"Good plan. That was my only question." He glanced at the pillows in her hand and smiled. "But thanks for bringing those. Never did like the blow-up kind." He picked up the stacked items and started down the trail.

Oh, that smile. Got her every time. And his nonchalant comment about the pillows... She struggled to breathe normally as she followed him back to camp. The mustangs and cougar had been amazing, but she had a feeling the excitement of that experience would pale next to the adventure awaiting her tonight.

Chapter Nine

By the time Austin and Drew returned to camp, the temperature had dropped enough that they both pulled out sweatshirts from their duffels. Austin chopped wood while Drew used the kindling he'd gathered to start a fire. Once he'd added a few larger branches, they had a decent blaze going. He helped her pull the log bench a little closer to it.

"Nice." She stood back and surveyed the setup. "If you want to begin cooking, I'll get us started with wine and the box of crackers I brought."

"Dinner's already made."

Her eyebrows lifted. "It is?"

"I cooked up a big batch of stew today. Left most of it for Rosie, Herb and Jonah, but the rest is in a pot that can go right on the stove."

"Efficient." Laughter danced in her eyes.

He knew what she was thinking and she was partly

right. He didn't want to waste a lot of time on food prep. While he set up the stove and started reheating the stew, she poured the wine and took a box of crackers out of a canvas bag.

She handed him a plastic goblet when he came over, and he tapped it against hers. "To the mustangs."

"To the mustangs." She took a sip. "Ah." Then she put her cup on the ground, opened the crackers and held out the box. "Hors d'oeuvres."

"Perfect." He sat on the log and took a handful because if he didn't, he was liable to reach for her instead. Once he did that, the whole program would go off the rails.

"This is the life." Setting the box of crackers on the ground between them, she reached inside the neck of her shirt and tugged out her necklace .

Next she pulled off her cap and the elastic band holding her ponytail and laid them beside her. Her hair tumbled to her shoulders and she rubbed her fingers briskly against her scalp until her hair stood out in wild and unbelievably sexy disarray.

He longed to bury his fingers in it and kiss her full mouth... No, they needed food. Food first. Fun later.

She picked up her wine again. "I probably look like Medusa."

"Not even close."

"Anyway, I'll dig up a brush in a little bit and tame this mess."

"Don't do it on my account. I like it that way."

She laughed. "Thanks for saying such a nice thing about my ratty hair. After a few hours of the cap and scrunchie I feel like I've been wearing a football helmet."

"Did you ever?"

"Yes, as a matter of fact. When I aged out of youth hockey I managed to get on the football team as the place kicker. My parents refused to sign the form so I could do kickoffs and field goals. They just knew I'd be sacked and maimed in some way."

He shuddered at the thought of her being tackled by six or seven hefty linemen. "In their shoes, I probably wouldn't have signed it, either."

She sighed. "There were times I wanted to be a boy." She glanced at him. "But right now I'm very glad I'm a girl."

"That makes two of us." He started to reach for the crackers again because kissing her was becoming an obsession.

"Your stew is bubbling."

"Oops." He put down his wine and stood. "Forgot I left it on high."

"You should let me tend it for a while so you can relax."

"No, ma'am." He turned down the heat and stirred the mixture. Fortunately, it hadn't stuck to the bottom. "I signed on to this expedition as the resident cook and Sherpa. Anyway, the stew will be ready before you know it."

"I find it interesting that this time you made dinner in advance." There was a definite teasing note in her voice.

"You probably think I wanted to leave more time for fooling around."

"Yes."

"I do, but also last night I was determined to impress you with my cooking skills. Tonight I don't feel the need to show off and create it in front of you."

"Because you intend to impress me in other ways?"

He looked over his shoulder. Her impish grin tested his restraint and he figured she knew it would. But two could play that game. "Yes, ma'am, I surely do."

"Oh, good grief. Don't try to tell me that cowboys are naturally more virile than other guys."

"I wasn't planning to tell you." He wanted to deliver the next line straight but he almost blew it by laughing. "I was planning to show you."

She groaned in obvious exasperation. "Okay, okay. Stop. You win."

"Allow me to point out that you started it."

"I did, and now I realize how quickly that kind of sexy talk gets out of hand. See, this is why I've never brought a date on a video trip."

"Never?" He looked at her in surprise.

"Never."

"I'm honored."

"You may end up being the first and the last. What happens when our camp is overrun by critters because we're too involved to notice?"

"That won't happen on my watch." He turned off the stove. "I want this trip to go well. I'm hoping we can camp again sometime soon, maybe after the wedding. I want to come back and get another look at those horses."

She gazed at him. "I'd like that, too. Obviously, you appreciate their value."

"They're incredible." So was she, with her wild hair and a sparkle in her dark eyes. If she had makeup on, he couldn't tell. He imagined she might look this way after waking up… He swallowed. "Stew's ready."

She pushed up from the log. "I'll get bowls and spoons if you'll pour me a little more wine. Maybe it will mellow me out."

He decided not to mention that the wine hadn't calmed either of them down the night before. If anything, it had lowered their inhibitions. But despite that, he'd make sure they didn't ignore the basic rules of safe camping because they'd become swamped by their emotions. Before they turned in for the night, the fire would be out and the food would be strung from a tree branch.

Once they were both seated again, with bowls of stew, more wine and the box of crackers between them, he glanced over at her. "I can't speak for you, but I've had a great time so far." He thought it was important to say so before they crawled into that tent. He wanted to establish that the trip was about more than sexual attraction.

"I've had a great time, too." She smiled at him. "How are your feet doing?"

"They're okay, but I need to buy some decent hiking boots for next time."

She paused with her spoon halfway to her mouth. "You'd do that?"

"Absolutely. I'll get some the minute I have a chance to shop for them. Might be after the wedding, though."

"Understood, but if you need help choosing, just holler." She took a bite of stew.

"Are you offering to go with me?"

"Yes, I'd go with you. And by the way, this is delicious."

"Thank you." He ate a spoonful of stew and it tasted even better than when he'd sampled it in Rosie's kitchen. "I admit that for the first part of the afternoon I thought hiking wasn't for me, but I've changed my mind."

"How come?"

"It's the best way to see the mustangs, for one thing. But on the way back I started thinking about trails that are too narrow for a horse but they lead to fantastic views. You've been on some of them."

"How do you know?" She took another bite of her dinner.

"I checked out your website on Rosie's computer

today. First I looked at the mustang videos, but then I found the ones you've taken around here and in Montana. Spectacular."

"Thanks. Last week I sold one to a company that does nature videos."

"Hey, that's great!"

"It is, actually. I'd submitted some before but they weren't interested. This one grabbed them and I've analyzed why that might be, so I can make similar but different ones they might take."

"Excellent plan."

"It's exciting to think about." Her expression grew animated. "Being on their site means I'll reach more people who for one reason or another can't experience nature personally. I'll be able to bring it right into their homes, offices, even schools."

Her enthusiasm for sharing what she filmed touched him. "And what about the folks who will see it and be inspired to go on hikes themselves? You'll be like a nature ambassador."

"I know! I love that. And potentially it could be a good revenue source. I get a percentage of every sale they make from their site. The more I have up there, the bigger those checks will be."

"We should toast that." He picked up his wine glass. "To more video sales."

She touched her glass to his. "And the amazing scenery that makes them possible."

He drank deeply from his wine glass and put it down. "Now I really want those hiking boots so I can be your Sherpa on a regular basis." The future looked bright.

"The only thing is, we're nearing the end of the season for getting good shots."

"I don't see why. You had some great winter stuff on

your site. I loved the one of frozen lakes and waterfalls, blankets of snow over a meadow, the Bighorns covered with snow. Gorgeous."

"It's pretty, but the operative word here is *frozen*. The winter landscape tends to be static. Wildlife is scarce. The episode I sold to them has lots of movement."

"Makes sense, I guess. It's video, after all."

"I had that lightbulb moment when the company chose to buy this particular one. I made it in June when I drove over to Cody to take footage of the rapids, some of it from a raft. I risked dunking my equipment but I lucked out, partly because I had an experienced rafting guide who watched out for me."

"Do you remember the name of the guide?"

"I vaguely remember it was an Irish name, although he wasn't from Ireland. Do you know someone who guides river rafting trips over there?"

"I do, but it would be too much of a coincidence if you got Liam."

"What's his full name?"

"Liam Magee. He's one of my foster brothers."

"That's him! Wow. What are the chances?"

"Well, I do have a lot of brothers." But he saw this as another positive sign that his relationship with Drew was meant to be.

"Liam is terrific. So personable and very good at what he does. Will he be at the wedding?"

"Yes, ma'am. Liam and his brother Grady will be there, along with their wives, Hope and Sapphire. Liam will get a kick out of seeing you again."

"I can't wait to see him again, either, so I can tell him about selling that project. It's very cool that he's your foster brother."

"Sure is." He couldn't wait for this weekend when

she'd meet several more of his brothers. By spending time with his family she'd realize how well she fit in.

But he was a little disappointed that she planned to stop making nature videos until the weather warmed up. He'd been looking forward to helping her. "How soon next spring do you figure you can start filming?"

"Depends on when we get our first thaw. Talking with you has given me an idea, though. If I took a few weeks in the winter and traveled south, I could still get some action shots."

"I guess that's true."

"I'm only part time at the college, so I might be able to leave between the end of my fall class at the college and the start of my spring one."

"True." Her trip would last over the holidays. He'd been looking forward to his first Christmas at home and she quite possibly wouldn't be around. Bummer.

She rested a hand on his thigh. "Don't look so sad. It's not like I'm leaving tomorrow."

He thought she might remove her hand, but instead she rubbed it lazily back and forth. He sucked in a breath. "Drew…"

"I've finished my dinner. Have you finished yours?"

He had no idea, but when he glanced into his bowl it was empty. So was his wineglass. "Seems like I have."

"How long do you think it'll take to critter-proof the camp?"

His pulse kicked into overdrive. "Five minutes."

Chapter Ten

Drew thought Austin was kidding about those five minutes. But she was astounded at how quickly the two of them had the dishes rinsed and put in one bag, the perishables in another with a cold pack and the nonperishables in a third bag. Apparently, they were both highly motivated.

He picked up the bags and the rope. "I'll hang these up if you'll smother the fire."

"Got it."

He started to grab the lantern and paused. "Will you be okay if I take this?"

"Sure. I'll stay right by the fire." She crouched beside it. Because they hadn't added any more wood, the blaze had been reduced to a few coals. She covered them with dirt and stirred the embers with a stick to make sure they were all out.

Starlight bathed the campsite in a silver glow and a

breeze whispered through the pines like a lover's sigh. The flurry of activity after dinner had kept her from thinking, but now she had a moment alone and she trembled with nervous excitement. The first time with a man could be wonderful, awful or somewhere in between.

Austin had joked about his amazing virility and she was inclined to believe he spoke the truth. But she'd never shared her tent with anyone, let alone a cowboy who loomed large and potent in her mind. After poking each blackened ember with the stick and getting no sparks, she tossed the stick away and stood to scan the tree line.

A light bobbed in the darkness as Austin walked back toward the camp. Her heartbeat nearly deafened her. She took a deep breath and tried to convince herself that tonight was no big deal. She'd been with guys before. But not this one. Not this muscled god of a cowboy who could arouse her with a glance.

When he was still several yards away, he stuck the lantern under his chin in a *Blair Witch Project* move. Helpless laughter swept through her, taking with it her case of nerves. As he stood in front of her grinning, she gasped for air. "I can't believe you did that."

"Had to. I could tell from your body language you were wound tight as a new rope." Nudging back his hat, he set down the lantern and pulled her into his arms. "I want you to be relaxed and happy."

"I'm happy."

"That's a start." He lowered his head and claimed her mouth.

And then it was all right, more than all right. If he made love the way he kissed—slow and steady, with exactly the right amount of pressure and a seductive use of his tongue—tonight would be spectacular. She was in the arms of a man who knew what he was doing, and what he was doing softened her as easily as wax touched by flame.

Clutching his broad shoulders, she melted against him, her body curving to fit his solid chest and the proud jut of his erection. His kiss deepened and his tongue made it clear what he intended to happen once they were stretched out in that tent. Her body grew liquid and pliant in response.

She was so absorbed in his kiss that she didn't realize he'd reached under her clothes and unfastened her bra until it gave way. His big hands warmed her skin as he circled her waist and stroked upward to cup her breast. She leaned back, craving the sensation of his fingers flexing and his thumb brushing lazily over her nipple.

Lifting his mouth a fraction away from hers, he took a breath. "You feel like satin," he murmured, nibbling her lower lip as he fondled her. "I'll bet you feel like this all over."

Her breathing grew shallow and she tightened her grip on his shoulders. "Let's go into the—"

"We will." He outlined her mouth with the tip of his tongue. "But first…there's something…" Releasing her breast, he reached for the button on her jeans.

She gasped as he flicked it open "But shouldn't we—"

"Shh." He pulled down her zipper and slipped his hand inside her panties.

"Austin."

He groaned as his fingers eased smoothly into her wet channel. "So ready."

Her resistance ebbed away. "This…this is crazy."

"I know. Let me."

Of course she did. His knowing caress soon turned her bones to jelly but he held her close with one strong arm while he worked his magic. Her climax came quickly and his kisses muffled her cries.

While she quivered in the aftermath, he picked her up and carried her to the tent. Kneeling, he cradled her against his chest as he unzipped the front flap. Then he sat her gently on the blanket.

Dazed and still struggling to catch her breath, she gazed up at him in wonder. No man had ever taken direct charge of her pleasure and she was a little stunned by how easily he'd done it.

"Just a preview," he murmured. "Be right back." He returned in seconds with the lantern and set it beside him. Sitting back on his heels, he untied the laces on her hiking boots and took them off along with her heavy socks. When he'd tucked both her boots and socks inside the tent, he pulled her sweatshirt over her head and laid it on top of the boots. "What about your necklace?"

"I tuck it in a boot." She lifted it over her head. As she handed it to him, she decided it was time to be less of a bystander and more of a participant. "How about you?"

He grinned. "I'm not wearing a necklace." He tugged at the hem of her shirt.

She caught his hands. "You know I'm talking about your clothes. Let me finish so you can undress."

"But I'm having fun taking off your—"

"I'm sure you are, but I also want you naked, cowboy."

"Yes, ma'am." Pushing himself to his feet, he nudged off his running shoes and began unsnapping his shirt while he stood outside the tent.

"You can come in." She scooted over. "I can make room."

"If I get in there, I'll want to go back to working on your clothes instead of mine. I want you naked at least as much as I want myself in that condition and probably more. In point of fact, I don't have to be totally naked, but it's fairly necessary for you to be."

Just like that, she wanted him again. "I get your meaning." As she was about to take her top off, he leaned down and laid his hat brim up against his side of the tent.

She noticed that his shirt was hanging open, exposing that gorgeous chest. Grabbing a handful of the fabric, she tugged him closer. "But you could kiss me again to tide me over."

His voice roughened. "I could, couldn't I?" Dropping to his knees, he tunneled his fingers through her hair and tipped her head back. "Your mouth is one of my favorite places on your sweet body." He settled his lips over hers.

She kissed him back with more hunger than she'd thought herself capable of. Running her palms over his bare skin, she explored the territory she'd first seen when he'd been sprawled under the sink at Thunder Mountain. She'd wanted to do this then. Now she could rub her hands all over that broad expanse of impressive muscles and springy chest hair.

She could also make him groan when she pinched his taut nipples, and gasp when she brushed her knuckles over the tight denim of his fly.

Breathing hard, he ended the kiss. "You're a devil."

"And you like it."

"Yes, ma'am, I love it. But you're still wearing way too many clothes. Are you taking off that shirt and bra or do I have to?"

"I will." She made quick work of the job. "Better?"

"Almost." Reaching behind him, he moved the lantern into the tent. As the light fell on her, he sucked in a breath. "Wow."

She flushed under the heat of his stare. "Now you're

the one wearing too many clothes. You need to take care of that."

"In a minute." Leaning forward, he cupped the back of her head. Kissing her almost reverently, he guided her down to the blanket. Then his kisses moved to the curve of her neck, then the hollow of her throat. At last he raked his teeth gently over her breast until he captured her nipple in his mouth.

She felt the tug deep in her core. Arching into his caress, she whimpered with pleasure. Cradling a breast in each hand, he kissed, licked and nibbled until she was panting and writhing against the blanket.

"Oh, Drew." Continuing his seductive massage, he returned to her mouth and thrust his tongue inside as he nudged her thighs apart with his hips. Locked tight against her most sensitive spot, he began to rock.

Once again, she came apart in no time at all. He made it seem so easy, this matter of letting go. When she opened her eyes, his face was in shadow but she could tell he was smiling.

She smiled back. "I only asked for a kiss."

"I'm a guy who likes to overdeliver." He eased away from her. "But it really is time to get serious about this program. We've fooled around long enough." On his knees again, he took hold of the waistband of her jeans and pulled them off.

Her damp panties came with them and she lay stretched out before him in the glow of the lantern. As his gaze traveled over her, the look in his eyes made her feel like a goddess. She would remember it for a very long time.

At last he cleared his throat. "I had pictured this moment, but my imagination didn't begin to… I didn't dream… You're incredible, Drew."

"Thank you." Warmed by the sincerity in his gaze, she reached over and fingered the material of his shirt. "Are you going to allow me the privilege of looking at you?"

He gave her a crooked smile. "I wouldn't call that a privilege."

"I would. So please finish taking off your clothes."

"Yes, ma'am." He left the tent.

As she lay there impatiently waiting, she heard the faint hoot of an owl. All her solo camping trips had been about lying in the dark listening for those night sounds. This experience with Austin was completely different. She wasn't complaining.

Then he stepped into the tent, his bundle of clothes in one hand and not a single scrap of fabric on his sculpted body. She drank in the sight of him. Her imagination hadn't done him justice, either.

As for the most private part of his anatomy, she'd certainly underestimated in that department. She didn't often find herself speechless, but the sight of Austin's pride and joy swept her brain clean of everything except primitive need.

He turned and leaned down to zip the flap closed. Oh, baby. Her body tightened as she imagined cupping those firm buns while he made love to her. Whew.

Next he stooped and put his clothes on the floor of the tent before unzipping his duffel. She could guess what he was after, and that was confirmed by the rustle of foil and a ripping sound as a packet was opened.

She almost offered to put it on for him but she wasn't that bold yet. Another time. Eventually this ritual could become playful, but not tonight. His labored breathing telegraphed his eagerness. She was excited, too. Just because he'd given her pleasure didn't mean she wanted to forgo this ultimate connection.

She'd expected him to just go for it considering how long the lead-up had been. Instead he lay down on his side facing her and she rolled to her side, too.

He smoothed a hand over her shoulder. "I made a silly boast a while ago. Cowboys can get a little full of themselves sometimes, although if you tell anybody I said that, I'll deny it."

"My lips are sealed." Amazing how he could stroke her shoulder and she could feel a pleasant zing between her thighs.

Lifting his hand from her shoulder, he rubbed his knuckle over her mouth. "Sealing these lips would be a crime against nature. I look at them and think of you eating a ripe strawberry or sipping champagne. Last night I had a very erotic dream about your lips."

Desire hummed through her veins but if he wanted to draw out the suspense, it was fine with her. "Want to share?"

He smiled. "Maybe later, after we know each other a little better."

"Now you're teasing me."

"Let's just say that in my dream you were teasing me."

Desire gripped her in tight fingers. "I don't want to tease you right now. Is that what you're doing?"

"No, ma'am. I wanted to take a little time to explain that once we get started I might… I might not last as long as I'd like. That's part of why I decided to have some fun prior to the main event. I don't ever want to leave a lady feeling frustrated."

"No danger of that." She paused. "Make love to me, Austin."

"My pleasure." He moved between her thighs. "Do you want the light?"

"I like it. I want to see your face while you're loving

me." She stroked his broad chest and discovered it was damp. Holding himself in check hadn't been as easy as he'd made it seem.

"I want to be able to see yours. Twice now I've missed that experience." Slowly he moved his hips forward. "Talk to me, Drew. I don't want to hurt you."

"You're not." Her pulse raced as she absorbed the sensation of being completely and utterly filled. "It's good. Very...good."

"Then I'm going to hold still for a few seconds, get my second wind. I want this to be special."

"It already is." She ran both hands down his back and felt his muscles twitch in reaction. "Don't forget, this is my first time doing it in a tent."

"I did forget." Weight braced on his forearms, he leaned down and placed kisses on her forehead, cheeks and mouth. "Welcome to tent sex." He initiated an easy rhythm.

"Mmm." The friction felt delicious. "I didn't think it would be so different, but it is."

"I think so." He kept moving. "Beds have their place, but there's something elemental about a sexual connection when you're surrounded by trees and animals. You can slide into their rhythm and become part of it."

Looking up, she held his gaze as he loved her with sure, steady strokes. In the distance a wolf howled. Then another answered. Her heart raced as her climax hovered near. "Take...take me there. I want... Oh, yes...*yes.*" With a wild cry, she surrendered to a wave of passion.

Gasping her name, he followed her into the whirlwind of sensation and they clung to each other as they trembled from the force of it. As their breathing slowed, a breeze ruffled the tent and stirred the branches of the pines.

She reached up and cupped his face. "Tent sex rocks."

He smiled. "Knew you'd like it."

"I don't just like it. I love it."

Leaning down, he brushed his mouth over hers. "Even better."

Chapter Eleven

Austin slept better than he had since leaving New Zealand. Camping in the wilderness was part of the reason. But mostly he credited the woman curled against him, the one who'd been so pleased with the first round that she'd happily engaged in a second one after he'd recovered his mojo. They'd heated up that tent good and proper.

Apparently in their semidrowsy state afterward, they'd each pulled a section of blanket around their bodies and cuddled together to ward off the cold. Early morning light filtered through their nylon shelter, and when a soft wind passed over them, it produced the effect of being underwater.

As he debated how long he could lie here before he'd want her again, he heard a noise outside the tent. He quickly recognized the sound of blunt teeth tearing at grass, the thud of a hoof on the ground and a snort. He shook Drew's shoulder.

She mumbled something he couldn't distinguish.

Putting his mouth close to her ear, he shook her again. "Drew. Horses."

"Hmm?" She rolled toward him, looking sexy and rumpled.

He wanted to kiss her in the worst way, but she wouldn't thank him if he did. Instead of kissing, she'd want to take a look outside. "Listen."

She lay still and then her eyes widened.

He kept his voice low. "What now?"

"Stay here."

"What about the hundred-foot rule?"

"I can't help it if they came to our front door." Moving carefully, she put on her clothes. Then she retrieved her small camcorder from her backpack and slowly unzipped the tent flap.

He held his breath as she slipped outside, but the lazy sound of horses grazing didn't change. Dressing as quietly as possible, he kept pausing to listen. He wasn't going out there, but he wanted to be ready if she needed him.

After about ten minutes, she poked her head into the tent. "They're starting to move off," she murmured. "I'm going to follow them as far as the trees. Want to come along?"

"You bet." He crept out into the cold, pale dawn. At first he scanned the ground for loose sticks that might crack in two if he stepped on them. The way was clear so he moved cautiously toward where Drew stood with her camera trained on the herd.

The mustangs had left the camping area, but they were close enough that he could pick out details—a scar on a flank, burrs tangled in a mane, a fresh scrape on a nose. They didn't carry an ounce of fat. Anyone who knew horses would be able to tell that they were as wild as the predators who stalked them.

They drifted slowly toward the line of tall pines, grazing as they went. The stallion stood apart, his attention on the humans. He snorted and pawed the ground.

Drew lowered her camera. "Let's go," she said in an undertone.

Austin nodded and they slowly retreated to their camping site. When he looked back, the horses had moved closer to the trees and the stallion was grazing.

Drew turned around, too, and sighed in relief. "That's better. I had the feeling that if I kept filming, the stallion wouldn't eat. He doesn't know that this funny black thing I'm holding is harmless." She set it on the log next to the fire circle.

"It's probably better if they don't get too comfortable around humans."

"So true." Her dark eyes shone. "But, Austin, I got some *amazing* footage. Between these close-ups and the cougar episode, I'd count this as my best outing ever."

"Good." She looked so beautiful in the soft light of dawn that it made his throat hurt. Her unbound hair was still tousled from their lovemaking the night before, which reminded him of the intense pleasure of sinking into her warm body. Naturally that affected his package.

As if she could read his thoughts, her cheeks turned pink. Then she smiled. "You know what?"

"What?" His voice was a rusty croak.

"I feel like celebrating."

"Thank God." Lacing his fingers through hers, he led her quickly back to the tent. After they crawled in, they had a bit of a rodeo getting their clothes off and they were laughing by the time they managed it.

"The one disadvantage of tent camping." He gathered

her close and groaned. "You feel so great. I want to kiss you all over but I can't."

She snuggled against him. "Why not?"

"Scratchy beard."

"Then it's my turn. Lie back."

Only a fool would disobey that order. He rolled over, bringing her with him. And...dear God, he was in heaven. She nibbled and licked until he thought he would lose his mind. As if her moist kisses weren't enough to drive him wild, her silken hair caressed his skin everywhere she traveled on her erotic journey. Finally, he begged her to fetch a condom from his duffel.

She wanted to put it on him and he was grateful. He was shaking so much he might have fumbled the job. She didn't waste any time doing it, either, which was a blessing because he was fighting for control. Then she was there, taking him deep as she gazed into his eyes.

His breath caught. This moment would be burned into his memory forever. Then she began to move, and the world became a dazzling blur of color and sensation. He tried to hold back, but it was no use. She took him over the edge and followed right after, her cries mingling with his.

When he stopped gasping and was able to focus on his surroundings again, he discovered her braced above him on her outstretched arms. She looked extremely pleased with herself.

Her soft chuckle was low and sexy. "Heck of a celebration."

He smiled. "Yes, ma'am. You sure know how to party." He dragged in a breath. "And now I'm gonna fix you breakfast."

"That would be nice." She combed a lock of hair back from his forehead. "I'll help."

"Ah, but it's my job, remember?" He captured her hand and nibbled on her fingers. "My excuse for tagging along."

"You can do most of it. But let's work on it together."

Oh, how he loved the way she was looking at him. And the way he felt when he was looking at her. He drew her head down and brushed his mouth over hers, careful not to scratch her with his beard. "That sounds great."

It was great, too. She loved the consistency of his scrambled eggs but he'd only brought salt and she preferred pepper. They compromised on the amount of ground coffee in the pot and made it too weak for him and too strong for her. They got their signals crossed as to who was watching the bacon and burned it. They ate it anyway.

The meal was far from perfect but the mood was. They straddled the log facing each other so they could touch knees and gaze into each other's eyes. It was a goofy thing to do but no one was there to see them acting like teenagers who'd just discovered how much they liked each other.

After the food was gone they continued to sit on the log talking about ways they could make the camping experience even better next time. He had no doubt there would be a next time. Visualizing the future, he saw a whole string of next times, whether they ended up camping or hanging out at her place.

Or they could stay at his place once he rented an apartment. Or…their place? Although he knew not to anticipate something so major this early in the relationship, he couldn't help it.

She'd worn her necklace outside her shirt this morning since they wouldn't be hiking. Reaching over, he took the pendant between his fingers. "Your grandmother had great taste."

"I know. She didn't just buy this in a store. She had someone design it."

He smoothed his thumb over the large pearl. "Then she must have had an idea of how she wanted it to look."

"Definitely. And it all has meaning. The pearl is so I'll remember to be kind to everyone because under their protective shell could be a pearl."

"I like that. What about the diamonds?"

"She used to say I was her sparkly girl and she never wanted me to lose my sparkle."

Tugging gently on the necklace, he brought her closer and looked into her eyes. "You haven't. I can see that sparkle right this minute."

She laughed. "I'll bet you can."

"What about the silver heart?"

"That's the most important part of the necklace. She always told me that no matter what, I should follow my heart."

"I would have liked your grandma." He leaned in, eliminating the gap between them.

"She would have liked you, too." She sighed. "We should probably pack up."

"But we'll come back."

"I'd like that."

"Then we will." He kissed her gently, mindful of his stubble.

As they broke camp and lugged everything to her truck, he thought about the next few days filled with wedding activities. The events would present some challenges for finding private time, but he was ready to tackle the obstacles and look for hidden opportunities to be with her.

On the drive back he started with the immediate one, Cade's bachelor party that night. "Obviously, it cuts out dinner and most of the evening," he said. "And no telling how late that will go, but I could come by your place whenever it winds down. Would that work for you?"

She laughed. "Are you asking if you can show up at my door at two in the morning?"

"Yes, ma'am, I suppose it could be that late. When you put it that way, it's an imposition. Never mind."

"You can show up at my door anytime, cowboy." She continued to watch the road, but she reached over and squeezed his thigh. "Anytime at all."

Heat traveled straight to his groin. "Any more of that talk and I'll be looking for a little side road."

"I've been fantasizing about that ever since we left our camp."

He sighed. "But we really can't."

"No, we really can't. We'll already get back later than I expected."

He checked the time on his phone. "And by now the ranch house will be filling up with people from out of town. I should be there."

"Absolutely. And I have an editing job to finish."

"You do? I thought you'd wrapped up Lexi and Cade's video."

"I did. This is a family reunion I shot last weekend. Rosie recommended me for it. I have most of it done but I promised to show them a preliminary version this afternoon."

"Which means you'd be free tonight and I'm not." He couldn't miss that bachelor party, but he wouldn't have to stay until dawn, or even close to dawn.

She flashed him a smile. "Like I said, anytime."

"Count on me, then. I'll be there."

"I'll leave the light on."

That reminded him of the ribbing Cade had given him about being a cab with its roof light on. This situation with Drew didn't fit that analogy at all, though. So what if she was the first woman he'd dated since he'd come back to town? He'd just been extremely lucky to find his soul mate immediately. Sometimes life happened that way.

He looked over at Drew. "Speaking of editing, how soon will you work on the video you took yesterday of the mustangs?"

"Since I won't be seeing you until late, I'll start on it after I finish the reunion one."

"Will you try to market it?"

"I might, although if I do, I'll give the profits to the folks who are doing so much to protect those horses."

"That's a great idea."

"Until now, I wasn't sure I had anything that would sell, but—" She paused as her phone chimed inside the console where she'd tucked it.

"Want me to get that for you?"

"That's okay. It's my sister texting me. I forgot that today she was supposed to hear whether she got an internship in Florence for the fall semester. If I find a good place to pull over, I'll stop for a minute and text her back."

"Florence, Italy?"

"Yep. She really wants the internship. It would be a great experience and it'd also look good on her résumé."

"Is she your only sister?"

"No, just the one closest in age to me. There are six of us, three and three. Like I said, big family. And that's only counting my siblings. The list of cousins goes on forever. No matter where you go in Billings, you're likely to run into a Martinelli. We show up in—" Her phone chimed again with a different tone. "Huh. Now she's calling. She must be really excited."

"There's a spot to pull over."

"I see it." She put on her blinker and moved to the side of the road. "I promise I won't be long." She switched off the engine and took her phone out of the console. "We both have things to do."

"Sure, but an internship in Florence is important stuff."

"It is, isn't it?" She dialed, put the phone to her ear and waited. "Hey, sis! Did you... Oh, no!" She listened for a moment. "I can't believe it." Turning to Austin, she gave him a thumbs-down sign. "They're idiots. Too bad for them." She paused. "I know. It sucks."

Even though Drew had the phone to her ear, Austin could hear her sister crying.

"Here's what we'll do." She met his gaze as she talked. "I'll come up and bring you down to Sheridan. You can be my assistant videographer for the wedding."

He took a deep breath and nodded to show he understood how her plan would impact them. If she needed to help her sister, he'd deal.

"Elise, it's absolutely okay," Drew said. "I could use the help and you know the routine. Meet me at Mom and Dad's and bring a suitcase. Tell Mom that I'll stop and pick up a pizza from the restaurant. Call it in for me, okay? Love you, too. Bye." She disconnected and looked at him. "I'm sorry."

"Don't worry about it. These things happen."

She smiled. "When it comes to my family, they happen *a lot* and if it were anything other than this, I wouldn't get involved. But Elise had her heart set on going to Italy and I can't just ignore her right now."

"Of course you can't."

"Thanks for understanding."

"Family's important." In fact, he was glad to see how much she loved hers. One more thing that proved how compatible they were.

Chapter Twelve

Drew had the rest of her day carefully structured. She'd finish the reunion video in two hours, tops. Then she'd shower and change, drive to Billings in time for dinner, and be back at her apartment with Elise before midnight. It was doable if she dropped Austin off and left immediately.

But when she swung her truck into the circular driveway in front of the ranch house, she realized any plans of a quick exit were down the drain. Rosie and Herb sat on the front porch with Jonah but joining them was her former rafting guide Liam Magee and a pretty blonde woman who must be his wife. Another couple was there as well, probably Liam's brother and sister-in-law.

Austin confirmed it. "Hey, it's Liam and Grady! Perfect. You can say hi to Liam now instead of in the middle of the wedding chaos."

"Quick, tell me the names of their wives again."

"Hope's the blonde with Liam and I think she just published a novel. The redhead is Sapphire, Grady's wife. He sculpts with recycled metal and she's a potter."

"Oh, my God. That's Grady Magee." Drew parked the truck and switched off the engine. "I didn't put it all together when you told me his name earlier, but I've heard of him. His work is in a gallery in Billings. Darn it, they all look like people I'd like to get to know better. I wish I didn't have to rush off."

"You'll probably have more time tomorrow after the rehearsal."

"Not really. I'll be shooting during the dinner, too. My method is to get more than enough and then pick out the gems."

"I see your point, but don't worry. There will be other chances in the future." Austin flashed her a smile as he opened his door. "I have a feeling you'll be hanging out with this family quite a bit."

His statement hit her like a splash of cold water. She'd meant to climb down herself to save time, but she was so startled by what he'd said that she was still sitting in the driver's seat when he opened her door. She wanted to ask what he'd meant by his remark, but now wasn't the time or place.

She let him help her down and automatically thanked him, but her mind was still busy with his comment. He could be referring to her growing friendship with the family through her work, but she didn't think so. His jaunty smile and his confident tone indicated that he saw her as becoming *part* of the family. And he'd be the connection.

Not that she didn't like him. She was crazy about him, in fact. But that didn't mean she was ready for the kind of commitment she thought he was hinting at. Maybe she was imagining things.

He must have sensed a change in her, though, because his smile faded. "Are you okay?"

"Just thinking about all I need to accomplish." Including a heart-to-heart with him, especially considering the imminent arrival of her sister. Good Lord, if Elise got the wrong impression of her relationship with Austin, that story would travel back to Billings. Her mother would start paging through wedding magazines and mailing Drew clippings of dresses and bouquets.

"Then let me grab my duffel out of the back while you head up to the porch. I won't bother with the stew pot and anything else I brought to cook with."

"Right. Just leave it. I'll get everything back to you tomorrow."

"Listen, you have my cell number if you need me for anything before then."

"Thanks. I appreciate it." She wished she didn't have this uneasy feeling that he'd misunderstood her intentions toward him. Now with Elise coming, she would have no opportunity to clear that up.

That said, the sooner she could talk with him, the better. She didn't want him giving his family the wrong impression about their relationship, either. But she couldn't do anything about the situation now and she really was excited to see Liam and meet his wife.

They left their chairs and came down the porch steps to greet her. "Isn't this a great coincidence?" Liam gave her a big grin and a hug. With his dark hair and green eyes, he could have been right at home in an Irish pub, except that he didn't have the accent.

"I'm so happy to see you again!" She hugged him back and then turned to meet Hope. When Drew mentioned hearing something about a novel, Hope lit up. Once again, Drew was sorry she couldn't stay longer and find out more about it.

She climbed the porch steps with them and was introduced to Grady and Sapphire, who were also extremely friendly and complimented her on the video she'd done for Thunder Mountain Academy, the residential equine education center for teens. That turned out to be a perfect lead-in to her news about selling the video she'd made while a passenger in Liam's river raft.

Rosie and Herb were also eager to hear all about it. When Austin came up the steps carrying his duffel, Rosie insisted that everyone should have a seat while she and Herb went to fetch snacks. There was no stopping Rosie when she launched into hostess mode, so in less than five minutes Drew was drinking lemonade and eating peanut butter cookies while participating in an animated discussion of the best way to market creative work.

The gabfest was wonderful and could have gone on for hours. Drew enjoyed every minute but knew she'd have to make her excuses soon or her whole plan would collapse. Finding the right spot to slip in a comment about leaving wasn't easy, though.

Then Austin did it for her. "I'll bet Drew hates to take off in the middle of this, but we need to let her go. She has a work deadline."

She sent him a look of gratitude. "He's right, I do. I have to finish editing the Hayworth family reunion video by four this afternoon. And thank you, Rosie, for getting me that gig. It was wonderful."

"The Hayworths are good people," Rosie said.

"They're terrific and they'd be okay if I took another day or two. But I need to get it done now because something else has come up I need to tell you about. I've asked my sister Elise to be my assistant while I'm shooting the wedding. She's done it before and she's a huge help."

Rosie beamed with pleasure. "What a wonderful idea! I can't wait to meet her. When will she arrive?"

"Actually, I'm driving up to get her tonight. So I really do need to leave." She picked up her glass. "I'll just take this into the—"

"I've got it." Austin smiled as he took her glass.

"Thank you. And thanks for being my Sherpa."

"My pleasure."

Turning, she bid everyone goodbye.

"I'll walk you to—"

"That's okay. Gotta run." She dashed down the porch steps. If she let him walk her to the truck he was liable to give her a quick kiss goodbye. Yes, they'd be on the opposite side of the vehicle, somewhat out of sight of the folks on the porch. But it was broad daylight and everyone would be able to see enough to know what was going on. She wasn't ready for PDA.

What was she ready for? She debated that question on the drive to her apartment. When it had been just the two of them at the campground, she'd let herself enjoy the freedom of having a sexy interlude that her family didn't have to know about. She'd been less guarded with him than the men she'd dated in Billings because he wouldn't be running into one of her relatives on the street.

Instead she'd be running into *his* relatives. She hadn't factored that into the equation. Now that she thought about it, all the Thunder Mountain guys she'd met either had wives or serious girlfriends. She hadn't been introduced to any who weren't in a committed relationship except Austin and his friend Jonah.

If finding a soul mate was a common trend in this group, she didn't want to be a part of it. But had she said anything that would lead Austin to believe she was looking for a permanent arrangement? Whether she had or not, they'd work things out the next time they had a chance to talk in private. In the meantime, she had a schedule to keep.

By sticking to that schedule, she pulled into the driveway of her parents' two-story frame house a little after six. She'd picked up the pizza her sister had ordered from the family restaurant, an extra-large called Everything but the Kitchen Sink.

On the drive from the restaurant it had filled her truck's cab with delicious aromas and she was starving. Other than lemonade and cookies at Thunder Mountain, she hadn't eaten since breakfast.

Elise came out to meet her with arms open wide. She'd had her dark hair cut in an asymmetrical style that was very artsy. "You are the best big sister a girl could ever have." She gave Drew a tight hug. "Mom and Dad mean well, but they're trying to help me find alternatives. They've been on the phone with all the aunts and uncles discussing it."

"Let me guess." Drew returned her hug. "You're not in the mood to consider alternatives."

"Bingo. I want to wallow in my misery. They can discuss and debate this if they want, but I'm taking turns ignoring them or offering ridiculous options." She grinned. "That frustrates the heck out of everybody, so it's probably a good thing you're getting me out of town."

"I had a feeling you'd be ready for a change of scenery."

"And pizza. I'm ready for pizza. It smells amazing. I'll carry it in, okay?"

"Be my guest." Drew was encouraged that Elise had

an appetite. She was slim to begin with, so she couldn't afford to skip too many meals.

Elise took the pizza from the passenger seat and closed the door. "You know what the worst part is? I almost got it. I'm the runner-up. Some master's student from Seton Hill got it, but I'm in second place. Big whoop."

Drew followed her sister up the walkway where they used to play hopscotch. "But that means if he or she can't go—"

"Oh, she'll go. If she applied for it, she has her ducks in a row. Who wouldn't?"

"I hear what you're saying, but stuff happens. Until the boat sails, or the plane takes off, you still have a shot."

"I suppose." Elise climbed the steps to the wide front porch. The wicker rockers that would be taken in with the first snowfall had patriotic cushions for the approach of Labor Day. "But it almost hurts worse if I nurture that hope. And wanting that means I'd like the woman who got it to have something major happen to keep her from going, which would be terrible for her. It's bad karma to wish for that."

"You're right. But you see, I don't care about her. I care about you."

"I know." Elise gave her a warm smile. "That's why I called you first. Where were you when you called back? I heard a lot of road noise."

"I was…" She opened the front door and heard a familiar sound, her mom on the phone and her dad commenting animatedly in the background. "Oh, boy."

"It's been like this all day, except for brief lulls when they both want to discuss what Aunt Fran suggested or Uncle Sid thinks I should do. Then there are Mom and Dad's recommendations."

"I'm surprised you're not twirly-eyed."

"Ah, I shrug it off. But it'll be nice not to listen to it for a few days."

Drew had only been home once since moving to Sheridan and that had been over Easter. Now she was reminded why. She reached for Elise's arm to pull her back so they could take the food and sneak over to Elise's apartment, instead. She'd have another pizza delivered to her parents. But she didn't move fast enough.

Elise breezed into the kitchen carrying the pizza. "Drew's here."

"Thank God!" Her mom quickly disconnected the call with "Drew's here" and hurried over to hug her. "You're just the person we need. Your sister has so many options now that the internship is down the drain, and she needs to narrow the list and pick something before the semester starts. Talk some sense into her."

Drew gazed at her dark-eyed mother, who kept her hair the same ebony shade it had been when she was twenty-five. Plump and vivacious, she had an Italian ancestry to rival her husband's. They were perfectly matched. They both loved food and a juicy emotional crisis. Now that the pizza was here, they could have both.

Drew adored them but never cared to live within a hundred miles of her folks ever again. "What do you say we have dinner first?"

"Excellent plan." Elise plopped the to-go box in the middle of the kitchen table.

Drew headed for the cupboard. "I'll get plates."

"I'll get wine." Her father bounded down the basement steps to the little wine cellar he was inordinately proud of.

"So we'll talk and eat." Her mother got out napkins and silverware. "But taking Elise down to Sheridan isn't a very good idea right now. If she stays in Billings she can start following up on some of these leads. Sid thinks he can pull some strings and get her an internship at an art gallery in the LA area. It wouldn't pay anything, but he knows a family over there who would give her a room for next to nothing."

"Or I could live on the beach." Elise started dishing pizza onto plates. "And pick oranges off people's trees. That sounds like fun."

Their father returned with a bottle of wine. "I don't think you're taking this seriously enough, honey." He plucked a corkscrew from a drawer and opened the bottle with the ease of a master.

"Drew thinks I shouldn't give up on Florence." Elise glanced over at her. "Right?"

"At least not for a few days. I mean, you're the runner-up. Until you know for sure the other person is all set, you—"

"Of course that person is all set," her mother said. "Who wouldn't be? Elise needs to move on, locate a similar position somewhere else, and the sooner the better. Serena is checking on possibilities in New York and Al has a connection with a very prestigious gallery in Cincinnati."

"But Elise needs to intern at a museum, not a gallery."

Elise pointed a wedge of pizza in her direction. "Exactly. And a European museum has far more cachet. So maybe I should book a flight to Italy and hang around Florence looking pitiful. They'll feel sorry for me and decide they need two interns."

Her mom looked aghast. "You wouldn't actually do such a thing, would you?"

Elise shrugged and turned to Drew. "I might. What do you think I should do?"

"I think you should finish eating so we can leave for Sheridan."

Her mom put down her wineglass. "Hold on a minute. I—"

"She just found out today." Drew laid her hand on her mother's arm. "She needs time to get her head around this so she can make a responsible decision."

Her mom glanced at Elise. "Do you?"

Right on cue, Elise's face grew solemn. "Yes. Yes, I certainly do."

"All right, then. We'll brainstorm while you're gone. I'll text you if anything comes up that you need to know about."

Drew shook her head. "That won't work, Mom. She'll be busy helping me with this wedding. It's a big deal and I don't want her to be distracted."

Her mother didn't look happy but she nodded. "We'll just get right on it the minute you get back, then."

"Sure." Elise gave her mom a quick smile.

Drew sighed in relief. Her mercy mission to rescue her sister from a weekend of hell had succeeded. That felt good.

Chapter Thirteen

Austin had looked forward to Cade's bachelor party as much, if not more, than the wedding. At Cade's request, the foster brothers had gathered around the fire pit in the meadow a short walk from the house. For many years, the meadow and the log cabins forming a semicircle behind the fire pit had been their sanctuary.

When Austin had come to live at Thunder Mountain, only three cabins had been here. He'd stayed up at the ranch house the first year because he'd been so young, but then he'd graduated to the cabins. Recently a fourth cabin had been added to expand the sleeping space for the academy students. Normally the teens would be living in the meadow, but the wedding had been scheduled during the break between the summer and fall semesters.

The menu for the night was simple—steak, baked potatoes, beans and beer. Cowboy chow. Austin had been part of the two-man team cooking the steaks. The other chef was Jake Ramsey, a firefighter who'd learned to fix hearty meals for a bunch of guys while on duty at the station.

Finn O'Roarke, who'd flown in from Seattle with his wife, Chelsea, made sure an iced tub of beer remained stocked with his signature brew, O'Roarke's Pale Ale. Several brothers had chopped enough wood to keep the fire going all night once the food was cooked. Now that Drew had other plans, Austin was willing to turn the party into an all-nighter.

The wives and fiancées were up at the house having their own event, leaving the meadow to the men. It was like old times, with their foster father, Herb, rounding out the group to an even dozen. And just like old times, the talk was mostly about women.

Everyone who wasn't in the know wanted to hear Zeke Rafferty's story. Of all of them, he'd been the least likely to marry and settle down. Yet tonight his fiancée, Tess, four months pregnant with their son, was up at the house with the other ladies. The wedding would take place next month and Zeke looked like he couldn't wait.

"I never thought I'd say this out loud, but babies rock." Zeke took a swallow of his beer. "I can't walk past a display of stuffed animals anymore without buying one."

"I hear you, bro." Damon Harrison's daughter had just turned eight months. "We finally bought a hammock for Sophie's room so we had a place to put 'em all. We're way past the teddy bear stage. Or the mammal stage, for that matter. She just got a plush tarantula from her uncle Zeke."

Finn shuddered. "Way to traumatize the baby, Zeke."

"Are you kidding?" He laughed. "She loves it. Nothing scares Sophie."

"I won't let her bring it to the wedding, though,"

Damon said. "Wouldn't want Finn to run screaming out of the barn."

"No, no, have her bring it," Austin said. "I guarantee Drew would love a video of that little cherub scaring Uncle Finn with a stuffed tarantula."

"Yeah, I wanna see that," Jake said. "Definitely YouTube worthy. I can't wait to have a kid. What kind of pregnancy kit is the best?"

Recommendations started flying around, and Austin wondered if he should be taking notes. He'd need to know this eventually. No worries. He'd ask when the time came.

He had plenty of other questions, though. Cade might need this info, too, come to think of it. So he forged on for Cade's sake. "What's the recommended time to wait before having your first baby?"

"Whatever it is," Zeke said, "we blew that call. We got pregnant by accident and didn't figure out until later that we were meant for each other."

"That's called divine intervention," Jonah said.

Zeke laughed. "Don't pull that preacher talk on me. I knew you when you were a hell-raiser."

"Exactly why I asked him to officiate at my wedding," Cade said. "It seemed fitting. But I'm interested in Junior's question. Why do you want to know, little buddy?"

Austin had consumed enough beer that he didn't bother objecting to being called either *Junior* or *little buddy*. "I was asking for you. I thought you might want to know."

"I don't need to know." Cade gazed at Austin. "I freely admit that Lexi is in charge of that program. We'll start trying to get pregnant when she says so. She has to do the heavy lifting."

Finn raised his bottle in Cade's direction. "Wise decision, bro. Let me get you another brewski and we'll toast that comment. It's brilliant." He headed off to the tub of iced beer. "Who else needs a libation?"

"I do," Grady said. A chorus of requests followed Finn's progress over to the tub.

"I wouldn't mind another beer," Cade said, "But I want to dig a little deeper into Junior's question. He's way too focused on this topic considering he doesn't have a fiancée, let alone a wife."

"I don't have one now, but I have a hunch I will soon."

Cade groaned. "I was afraid that would be your answer."

"Never fear, old buddy." Austin gave him a light punch on the shoulder. "She's perfect. Yesterday she took me out to Bighorn Canyon to see the wild mustangs and we got along great."

"But wasn't that, like, your second date?" Jonah thanked Finn for the beer and opened it.

"Yeah," Austin said. "But when you go camping with someone you see the real person."

"There's some truth to that." Cade gazed at Austin. "But here's a bigger truth. Three days ago you didn't know she existed."

"So? Sometimes lightning strikes."

Brant Ellison, the only cowboy in the group who was bigger and more muscular than Austin, cleared his throat. "I know a guy who was actually struck by lightning. He was addlepated for days." Brant smiled at Austin. "You might want to rethink your metaphor."

"Or extend it." Ty Slater and Brant had been best friends while they lived at the ranch and still kept in close touch even though Ty was now a lawyer working in Cheyenne. "Let's say you were hit by lightning and she's the one for you. But it works two ways. She'd have to feel that lightning strike, too."

"She likes me. I know she does."

Damon sighed. "I hope you're not basing that on a few rounds of mattress bingo."

"I'm not! We have way more going for us. She wants to help me get my trail ride business going. She's offered to give me tips on the website design and do a video for it. She said I make her video expeditions easier because I carry most of the stuff. She likes my cooking."

Cade lifted his beer in Austin's direction. "You're ahead of me there, bro. But you're making me mighty nervous with this 'I have a hunch' talk."

"I'm crazy about her and I'm pretty sure she's crazy about me. I see no reason why we won't be engaged within a month or so."

Jonah choked on his beer and Cade groaned.

Austin glanced around at his brothers and they were all staring at him like he was one doughnut shy of a dozen. "What? When it's right, it's right. Life's short, so why waste time? Look at Rosie and Herb. Met, fell in love, got married, bam. That sure worked out okay."

Liam had been silent through the interchange but he finally spoke. "That's a good point, but Ty's right. You have to make sure Drew's on the same page, and I—" He paused. "Well, never mind. I shouldn't poke my nose in."

Austin felt a prick of unease. Liam had spent several days with Drew on that rafting trip and the guy had good instincts about people.

"Please poke your nose in," Cade said. "The rest of us have tried and we're getting nowhere."

"It's just that I got to know Drew fairly well on that rafting trip, and this afternoon on the porch I could tell you were over the moon, but I wasn't getting that level of intensity from her."

"That's because she wouldn't show it in front of everybody." But she had acted somewhat distant after his comment in the truck about spending a lot of time with his family in the future. "When it's just the two of us, she's very...um, affectionate."

Damon came over and put an arm around his shoulders. "I get that. I'm sure you had a rockin' good time in Bighorn Canyon. But you can't jump from that to a proposal without some indication she's thinking along the same lines as you."

"What sort of indication?"

Damon turned to the rest of them. "Indications. What you got?"

"She invites you over to help her trim her Christmas tree," Ty said. "That's what Whitney did. I loused it up, but that was her way of hinting she wanted to take things to the next level."

Damon nodded. "Any invitation into her space is a good sign. Phil invited me to stay at her house, although I didn't handle that opportunity well, either."

"See there?" Austin felt better. "She let me go along on her camping trip to see the mustangs."

Cade gazed at him. "Did you ask to go?"

"Well, yeah, but she was fine with it. Then today she said I was welcome at her place anytime."

"But whose idea was it to go over there?" Cade skewered him with a glance.

"Mine, but—"

"It really does need to be her idea," Jake said. "And even then, you can get your signals crossed, misinterpret what everything means. Has she taken the initiative on anything?"

Austin thought back over the past two days. He'd asked her out to begin with and then invited himself along on the camping trip. He'd suggested going over to her apartment after the bachelor party. "Maybe not. Oh, wait. She volunteered to go along when I bought hiking boots. That was totally her idea."

He considered it a positive sign, but when he took inventory of how it was being received by his brothers, several of them looked ready to bust out laughing. "Well, it's something, right?"

"It's something, all right," Damon said. "But I wouldn't go lining up a preacher based on a potential shopping trip for hiking boots."

"So you're all saying I should back off a little."

"Or a lot," Cade said. "Hell, Junior, your plane landed four days ago! I'll bet you're still jet-lagged."

"I have to back off for the rest of the weekend anyway. Drew's sister will be in town through Sunday."

Jonah clapped him on the back. "Divine intervention."

Austin considered it more of a monkey wrench in his plans than divine intervention, but he respected Drew's need to comfort her sister. Maybe it was a good thing he and Drew were forced to take a break this weekend. They'd be all the more eager to get together next week. But he might let her make the first move.

Drew ate two slices of pizza and then extricated herself and Elise from the house. She and Elise spent most of the drive talking about the wedding and Thunder Mountain Ranch.

"So let me get this straight." Elise scooted down and propped her feet on the dash, something she loved doing whenever she was in the passenger seat and her parents weren't around to chastise her for it. "First this couple took in foster boys and now they're running a coed equine academy for teens. They must be saints to want teenagers around all the time."

"I can't imagine it, either, but they seem to thrive on the constant activity."

"And I thought our family was crazy."

"Our family *is* crazy. Remember that these academy students aren't related. I think that makes a huge difference in the drama quotient."

"Yes, but you said the foster brothers consider themselves semirelated and quite a few of them are part of the mix, right?"

"They are." Drew pulled into her parking space at the apartment complex. "Which brings me to another subject. But let's wait until we get inside to talk about it."

"Is it top secret?" Elise sounded thrilled with the idea.

"Actually, yes." She unbuckled her seat belt and opened her door, which switched on the dome light. She turned to look at Elise. "Before I say anything, you have to pinkie-swear that you won't tell Mom and Dad."

"Ooh, sounds juicy. Are you pregnant?"

"God, no! Bite your tongue."

"It wouldn't be the end of the world. You're twenty-eight and you'd make a great mom."

Drew stared at her. "What makes you say that?"

"You're always taking care of people, like bringing me down here to cheer me up, as if you thought they were driving me nuts with their crazy-ass suggestions."

"Weren't they driving you nuts?"

Elise laughed. "Sort of, but it's like a game to me. They get all serious about my future so I tell them I'm going to be a beach bum. I like going for the shocking statement."

"You pull their chain on purpose?"

"Sometimes." Elise grinned at her. "When the devil in me can't resist. Family drama can be a spectator sport."

"No, it's not! It's distracting as hell!"

Elise blinked. "Not to me." She was quiet for a moment. "But I can see it bothers you. From now on I won't deliberately light any brush fires when you're around."

"Thank you." She gazed at her sister. "Are you saying you didn't really need rescuing?"

"Maybe not the way you thought."

"But you were crying."

"I know, and I was upset, but I'm over it." She reached out and squeezed Drew's shoulder. "That doesn't mean I'm not excited about spending the weekend with my big sis. Let's go in so I can find out what this major secret is about."

Drew locked the truck and led the way up the outside stairs to her second-floor apartment, all the while thinking she might have overreacted by inviting Elise down here. Elise hadn't asked to come, had she? And now there was the issue of Austin to deal with.

Her sister was too observant to miss the chemistry, so the relationship had to be explained before they drove out to Thunder Mountain Ranch the next day. Some sisterly advice from Elise might be helpful before Drew saw Austin again. Maybe Elise could help her figure out where Austin was coming from.

"I have to warn you," she said as she unlocked the door. "The apartment's even more Spartan than the one I had in Billings. My decorating consists of hanging up my Ansel Adams posters and my signed Wayne Gretzky photo."

"Works for me." Elise rolled her small overnight case into the living room, which contained a worn sofa on one side of the room and Drew's video equipment on the other, including a large flat screen, her computer, and various cameras, tripods and lights.

"I'll take the sofa and give you the bed." Drew felt the

need to offer even though she knew Elise would probably refuse.

"Are you kidding? I love sleeping on this sofa. I was
afraid you might have replaced it." She plopped down
on it and patted the cushions. "This sofa and I have a
history."

"You do, at that." Elise had spent the night on it several times, most notably when she'd been dumped by a
guy she'd been madly in love with.

"Are you gonna sit down and tell me the secret stuff
or what?"

"I am." She dropped her purse onto the desk beside
her computer. "After I get us some wine."

"Excellent." Elise kicked off her shoes and curled up
on the sofa. "I didn't drink much at Mom and Dad's."

"Obviously as the designated driver, neither did I."

Moments later as they sipped red wine from juice
glasses and snacked on trail mix, Drew gave her sister a
brief rundown on Austin.

"He sounds great."

"He is great unless he's hoping to lock down something permanent in the near future. If you could observe
the situation tomorrow and see if you pick up on that,
too, I'd appreciate it."

Elise grabbed another handful of trail mix. "Your instincts tell you he's getting serious, right?"

"Right, but—"

"Then you need to talk to him ASAP and relay your
concerns." She popped the trail mix into her mouth.

"But what if I'm wrong?" Drew's stomach tightened.
"Won't that seem arrogant to assume he's getting serious if he's not?"

Elise stopped chewing. "What if you're right? Wouldn't

you rather set the record straight before he goes any further down that road?"

"Yes, yes, I would."

"I wish Brian had been more honest with me instead of being afraid he'd hurt my feelings."

"Okay." Drew took a deep breath. "But there's all this wedding stuff going on so I'm not sure when I'll have a good opportunity until next week."

"I wouldn't wait that long if I were you. Is there a good coffee shop in town?"

"Rangeland Roasters."

"Then you could invite him to meet you there tomorrow morning."

"And leave you here by yourself? That's not right after I—"

"Listen, sis." Elise leveled a stern glance at her. "You came charging to my rescue when you thought I was in need. Maybe I wasn't as desperate as you thought, but I'm thrilled to get out of Billings for the weekend. If I weren't here, you could meet this guy, no problem."

"Except without your encouragement, I wonder if I would have set up a coffee date."

"Regardless, it's the right move, and I can certainly manage to amuse myself for a couple of hours while you have a heart-to-heart with your cowboy."

"It's after midnight. How can I invite him this late when we're talking about tomorrow morning?"

"Didn't you say he was at the bachelor party tonight?"

"Yes, but—"

"Text him. He'll be up."

"All right." Drew sent the text and his response came shooting back. He'd be at Rangeland Roasters at ten.

Elise gazed at her. "He's at a bachelor party with his foster brothers, where the booze is flowing and the laughter is loud, and yet he answered your text almost immediately. Any doubts that this conversation is necessary?"

Drew sighed. "Not a single one."

Chapter Fourteen

Austin borrowed Jonah's truck and arrived at Rangeland Roasters ten minutes early. After receiving Drew's text last night he'd almost shown it to Cade as proof that she was into him. In spite of having her sister staying with her, she wanted to see him. Even better, she'd asked him this time instead of everything being his idea.

But he'd decided not to tell Cade about the coffee date. He hadn't said anything about it to Jonah, either. He'd just mentioned an errand he needed to run in town. Jonah had been too groggy to ask questions, anyway. He'd just handed over his keys.

Most everyone had bunked down at the cabins although they hadn't packed it in until around four. Austin had stayed until the end, but he'd cut way back on his beer consumption so he wouldn't be hungover this morning. A shower, a shave and clean clothes had perked him up, although he'd felt a little weary on the drive in.

But now that he was seated at a table by the window and watching the door, an adrenaline rush counteracted his lack of sleep. When he caught sight of Drew, his pulse hammered. He imagined her thinking about the next couple of days without any time together. Maybe she'd decided to fix that problem because she plain liked being with him.

She caught sight of him through the window and waved. He lifted his hand in response. He loved the way she moved, the way her dark ponytail swung with each stride of her long legs. He loved that she was tall and not fussy in the way she dressed. Jeans and a scoop-necked T-shirt looked great on her. She wore the pendant necklace, like always.

Her grandmother had told her to follow her heart. Maybe that was the reason she was here. As she came through the door, he stood and waited for her. He hadn't been aware of smiling until she returned his smile.

"Thanks for meeting me." She stayed just out of reach as she pulled her wallet out of her purse. "My treat."

"Put your money away. It's on me." He was a little disappointed that she was keeping her distance, but Rangeland Roasters had become a gathering place for residents of the town and she might not want to advertise that they were involved.

"But I invited you."

"Let me pay." He stepped closer and lowered his voice. "And then let's get out of here."

"But—"

"Drew, I insist. What do you want?"

"Just regular coffee."

"Nothing to eat? A muffin? A Danish?"

"No, thanks, but go ahead if you're hungry. I'll hold the table."

"I thought I'd get it to go."

She looked uncertain and finally nodded. "Okay."

As he ordered the coffee, he thought about the side street where he'd parked. It was only a block off Main, but not much traffic went that way. He'd chosen the spot on purpose because he hadn't envisioned sitting in the coffee shop if they could go somewhere more private. He'd put the sunscreen over the windshield.

He used a cardboard carrier for the coffee and decided to get one blueberry muffin in case she changed her mind about eating something. When he came back she was standing next to the table as if still guarding it.

"I'm not sure where we could go," she said. "Maybe we should stay here."

"I'm parked a block away. We can sit in the truck."

"The ranch truck?"

He had a hunch why she'd asked. If they ended up making out a little bit and someone noticed a couple kissing in the truck, she wouldn't want it to be the one with the Thunder Mountain Academy logo on the side of it. He hoped they would kiss. This might be the only chance they'd have for a couple of days. "I brought Jonah's."

"Oh. All right, then."

He followed her to the door and managed to reach around and open it for her without spilling their drinks. She smelled more delicious than either the muffin or the coffee. "To the right." He fell into step beside her.

"How was the bachelor party?"

"Terrific. Like old times. How's your sister doing?"

"She'll be fine. I'm glad I suggested bringing her down here, though. Typical of them, my parents are trying to fix this and they're being a little pushy about it."

"Then I'm glad you fetched her. I was surprised to hear from you, though. Happy, but surprised."

"I decided we needed a chance to talk."

He chuckled. "Oh, yeah?" Then he gestured to the right again. "Down here. The dark blue truck at the end of the street."

"I see it."

"Where's yours?"

"On Main. I was lucky and found a spot close to Rangeland Roasters."

Obviously she hadn't been planning to invite him to sit in her truck. "Did you get that reunion video edited in time?"

"I did. Everything's under control."

"I wish I could say the same."

She glanced up at him. "What's wrong?"

"I desperately want to kiss you." He took the keys out of his pocket and stepped around her to unlock the passenger door. "But I know we need to wait until we're inside the truck. I can understand why you wouldn't want to advertise that we're together."

"Austin, I—"

"Just a kiss. I promise not to get carried away." He opened the door and once she was in, he handed her the cardboard tray with their coffee and the muffin. "You can set that on the dash."

"The console would be better."

He smiled. "Not if I'm going to kiss you." He closed the door and walked around to the driver's side, his heart pounding in anticipation. A mere twenty-four hours had passed since he'd held her yet it felt like weeks.

Before he climbed in, he tucked his hat behind the seat so it wouldn't get in the way. Then he noticed that their coffee tray sat on the console. That was a clear signal and his good mood evaporated. "You don't want me to kiss you."

"I do, but first we need to talk about something."

Last night's conversation with his brothers started playing in his head. He'd been so sure they were wrong and that Drew felt the way he did. He took a calming breath, settled behind the wheel and turned to face her. "Shoot."

Her expression softened. "I really like you."

"I really like you, too." He swallowed. "I have a feeling there's a *but* coming after that, though."

"Not really. It's more of a question. Just now you mentioned that we were *together.* Yesterday you said I'd probably be seeing a lot of your family in the future. Am I imagining things, or are you getting serious about me?"

That knocked the breath right out of him. He stared at her as he scrambled for what to say. His brothers were right. He was moving too fast and had jumped to conclusions based on her eagerness to make love to him.

"I think I have my answer," she said gently.

He scrubbed a hand over his face. "I feel like a damned fool. But yesterday you were so…so…"

"Willing?"

"Yes, ma'am. That's a good word for it."

"Then I'll take some of the blame for misleading you. I think I mentioned that in Billings, whenever I dated someone, it became common knowledge in my family pretty fast."

"You did." He didn't think what she was about to say would make him feel any better but he would hear her out. If nothing else, he could get his act together while she talked.

"You're the first man I've been with where I didn't have any comments from the peanut gallery. It was liberating."

Okay, that info made things way worse. "So you

would have been that *willing* with any joker who happened along?"

"No!" She gazed into his eyes, her expression earnest. "I said it wrong. I've been here nearly eight months and haven't gone out with anyone."

"Probably because you were too busy."

"I was busy, but I was asked out a couple of times and I wasn't motivated to date either of them. The minute I saw you under that sink I was a goner. If you hadn't asked me out I eventually would have asked you."

"So you're physically attracted to me?" He'd briefly dated a woman in New Zealand who'd only wanted sex from him. No conversation, no shared meals, no scenic drives.

"Of course I'm physically attracted but I also like you. You have a zest for life. You've had misfortune but you've risen above it. You set goals and achieve them. I admire all that."

"But you still have an issue."

"I like you very much, but I'm not in the market for something permanent."

"Ever?" His hopes and dreams circled the drain.

"I don't know about ever, but certainly not now. I left Billings to get away from family responsibilities that made me feel trapped. I need to figure out who I am and what I want. Selling that rafting video was huge and it could be a good direction for me. I won't know that for a while, though, and in the meantime…"

"You don't want some cowboy putting a halter on you." Cade and the rest of his brothers had nailed it. He wasn't giving up, but he'd better be careful or he'd scare her off.

She smiled. "That's about the size of it."

He had to ask the next question but he was worried

about how she'd answer. "Is this about dating other guys?"

"No."

His shoulders sagged in relief. "I'm glad, but sort of confused."

"Can't we just have fun?" She fiddled with her pendant, sliding it back and forth along the chain. "Why not leave it at that?"

Because he'd outgrown that phase in his life. He'd even told her so on their first date. He'd left New Zealand because that kind of loose arrangement didn't work for him anymore. He'd always preferred situations that had a trajectory, an end game.

Now that he'd found the right woman, he didn't want to waste time just hanging out. He wanted to make plans, create a blueprint for the future. But if he said any of that she was likely to get out of the truck and walk away.

Frustrating though it might be for him to back off and give her time, he had no choice. It was either do that or abandon the whole deal, which was another option. Logically he knew she wasn't the only woman in the world he could love.

But when he looked into her dark eyes with their silent plea for understanding, he couldn't think logically. Instead he pictured giving up the privilege of kissing those plump lips and the intense pleasure of holding her lithe body while they made love. Nope, he couldn't imagine ending everything because she didn't share his vision. Instead he'd have faith that someday she would.

She moistened her lips. "You're being very quiet over there."

"Just making sure I get it." He was focused on her mouth and the sheen on her lower lip where her tongue had swept over it. "We'll be exclusive but don't have any real claim on each other. I guess that means if it stops working for us we won't have to break up because we were never a unit in the first place."

"Exactly. Can you live with that kind of setup?"

"Yes, ma'am, I surely can." He glanced at the cups of coffee, which would be lukewarm by now, and the muffin, which certainly didn't interest him and might not interest her, either. "Want to drink the coffee or move it?"

"I vote for moving it. Meeting for coffee was just an excuse."

"Then allow me." Picking up the cardboard tray, he opened his door and climbed out so he could set it on the hood. Then he got back in the truck. "I'll deal with it later." He reached for her, coaxing her toward him even though they had the barrier of the console between them. "Right now I have more pressing concerns, like giving you a proper kiss."

She leaned over and wound her arms around his neck. Her necklace dangled between them. "An improper kiss will do."

"Don't know if I can manage that in such tight quarters." Cupping her cheek in one hand, he angled his body and settled his mouth over hers. The moment he touched those velvet lips he groaned in frustration.

She pulled back. "What?"

"I feel like I'm kissing you through the bars of a prison cell. I could rip this console out with my bare hands."

"It's not your truck."

"Good point." He released her. "I'm coming around to your side."

"Austin, there's not enough room."

He opened the door and glanced over his shoulder. "We'll make room." Once he opened the passenger door he got her to hold on to the dash and lift away from the seat. He slid underneath her and closed the door. "Now sit on my lap."

"This is a tight fit, Austin. We're not small people."

"No, but we're motivated people. Scoot around and kneel on the seat so you're facing me. Ah, that's better."

She sat on his knees and gazed into his eyes. "You've done this before."

"And you haven't?" He cradled her face in both hands.

"I didn't say that. Making out in truck cabs is part of a Montana teenager's education."

"Then kiss me, lady. Kiss me like you mean it."

"With pleasure, cowboy." She fit her mouth to his.

He swore rockets exploded when that happened. Maybe a car driving by had backfired, but he thought it was the effect of her tongue in his mouth and his tongue in hers. Their kiss was hotter than a campfire. When he reached under her shirt and unhooked her bra she didn't stop him.

But they were still in a public place in broad daylight, so he contented himself with stroking and fondling rather than pulling off her shirt so he could kiss her there, too. His package ached something fierce but he suffered in silence. Or mostly silence. He let out a moan or two.

When she pulled back she was gasping. "We need to stop. Otherwise…"

"Otherwise I'll have to drive you to a motel and that's not how I want our relationship to go."

"Me, either." She pressed his hand to her breast. "But I love it when you touch me."

"I love it more." He gave her a gentle squeeze. "When are you taking your sister home?"

"Sunday afternoon." She arched into his caress. "Ah, that's nice."

"So you'll be back here Sunday night?" He rolled her nipple between his thumb and forefinger.

"Uh-huh."

"Then let me know when you're home again. I'll come over."

"Great plan." She sighed. "I don't want to leave this truck."

"But you have to." With reluctance he fastened the front catch on her bra. "Did you wear this for me?"

"Yes."

"Thank you." He'd take all the encouragement he could get. If she'd worn this bra on purpose for their coffee date, then she'd hoped they'd end up like this, exchanging hot kisses in some secluded spot. She might be putting the brakes on when it came to making a commitment, but he didn't think she'd hold to that much longer.

Chapter Fifteen

Drew reported to Elise that lines had been drawn in the sand. But that hot interlude in the truck made her wonder how defined those lines were. After the way she'd kissed him, he had to know that whenever he was around, she was like a hand grenade with the pin pulled.

Now that she and Elise were on their way to the rehearsal and Elise would meet Austin, Drew felt the need to unburden herself. "I don't want to get serious about him, but when he touches me, I turn to jelly. That could be a problem."

"Are you telling me that if he proposed during a passionate moment you might say yes?"

"I hope not."

"But you're not sure."

"No."

"So don't be alone with him."

"I want to be alone with him. He's sizzling hot."

Elise threw up her hands. "Then marry the guy! He sounds perfect for you, so why fight it?"

"Because marriage is forever. It means in-laws and mortgages and likely it means babies. I'm not ready for that kind of total commitment."

"You may not be, but I'm ready to commit *you* somewhere if you keep this up. You need to decide what you want and stick to it no matter what."

"That's not so easy when Austin's around."

"Come on, Drew. He's just a guy."

"Say that again after you've seen him. He's gorgeous. And on top of that, he's sweet and generous and—"

"You sound like a woman in love."

"I'm not!"

"Are you sure, sis?"

"Yes." But she wasn't sure, and that made everything more confusing.

At the ranch, Drew made sure her sister met the members of Austin's family who were helping prepare for the big day. Then she introduced Elise to Austin when they went to the barn to set up the umbrella lights for the ceremony. He was one of the foster brothers in charge of bringing horses in from the pasture and putting them in their stalls for the rehearsal.

After he'd gone out the back door to fetch another pair, Elise glanced at Drew. "I get it. He's the stuff fantasies are made of."

"That's why I'm so glad you're here, so you can see what I'm up against."

Elise laughed. "In your shoes I'd be up against that cowboy as often as possible."

"Yeah, yeah." Drew set an umbrella light in place. "See if you can find a convenient socket for this baby."

"Got it." She shoved the plug into the outlet. Then

she glanced around to see if they were still alone. "It's the guy's attitude that I really like. He's modest, yet at the same time driven to succeed. Lately I've run into men who endlessly brag about themselves for no reason. They're like the old saying All Hat and No Cattle."

"I know. Austin's initiative turns me on. That's what makes this so complicated." Drew switched on the umbrella lights and one of the horses nickered.

"They really want the horses in here for the ceremony?"

"They do. Lexi's hired one of her riding students to come in tomorrow morning and braid ribbons into their manes so they'll look festive."

"I can't wait to see how this goes."

"Me, either. Hey, go stand where Cade and Lexi will be so I can get a reading." She adjusted the umbrella's tilt. "Looking good. We can start bringing everyone in. I need to mic Cade but otherwise we're in decent shape."

Elise walked back over to her. "Before we do that, let me ask you something. You told Austin where you're coming from, but are you clear about his thinking?"

"The look on his face when I asked if he was getting serious said it all."

"But there are different levels of serious. I know some couples that have been hanging out for years and they never moved in together, let alone married and had kids. They just like each other. Maybe that's all he's looking for."

"That would be great." She smiled at Elise. "Thanks for being here, sis. You're good moral support."

"Back atcha."

Drew took one last look around the barn to assess her lighting setup. "Okay, let's get this show on the road."

Walking to the open barn door, Elise made a megaphone of her hands. "Everyone can come in now! You first, Cade. Drew needs to mic you up."

Cade walked into the barn with a big smile on his face. "I feel like a celebrity."

"You are." Drew clipped the mic to his shirt. "You and Lexi are the stars of the show, but you're the easiest one to hide a mic on because you'll be wearing a jacket."

"And a vest." He fingered the mic's wire. "I might want to run this under the vest instead of under the jacket."

"Right, and I'm thinking I need to put one of your brothers in charge of getting this put on you tomorrow afternoon."

"Ask Damon to come in."

"He understands this stuff?"

"He's a contractor so I'm sure he can manage it. But he's also my oldest friend and I know he'd do it right."

"Then let's get him in here."

Cade went to the door and summoned Damon, who came in and informed them that the sound guys had arrived and wanted to set up.

"You can tell them that's fine." She was interested in seeing how the sound system would work in the barn.

Once Damon came back, he paid close attention to the correct way to attach the mic and the small battery pack. She felt confident she could hand the job over to him for the ceremony.

Damon glanced around at Drew's lighting installation and his brown eyes lit with approval. "You did a great job with the lighting."

"Thanks." Pleased with the compliment, Drew flashed him a smile. "We can let everyone else in now."

"I'll give them the all-clear." Damon left.

Moments later Lexi came in. After admiring the way her husband-to-be was wired for sound, she watched the speakers and amps being hooked up for the musical portion of the ceremony. "Cade, I think it's too elaborate. We don't need the equivalent of a symphony in here."

"It's our big day," Cade said. "We need a big sound."

"Music sets the tone." Jonah joined the discussion. "I'm glad you're testing it tonight. I've seen ceremonies rise and fall on the choice of music."

"I wanted a single guitar," Lexi said. "I was outvoted."

"Interesting idea." Jonah glanced toward the open door where Austin stood talking to Rosie and Herb. "I know we're at the zero hour, but if you change your mind, we have someone who plays guitar."

Lexi perked up. "I'd forgotten that! It's been a few years, but as I recall, he was pretty good."

"Austin plays guitar?" Drew couldn't have been more surprised.

"He doesn't tend to talk about it," Jonah said, "but he's got a nice touch. He picked it up while we were both living at the ranch and apparently played for sing-alongs when he guided trail rides over in New Zealand."

Drew looked over at Austin. She could imagine him with a guitar balanced on his thigh, now that she thought about it. It completed the picture, in a way. "Did he bring his guitar when he came back?"

"He did," Jonah said. "He considers guitar playing as his sideline. He plans to work it into his own trail rides."

"That's very cool."

"Speaking of sidelines," Elise said as she gazed at Jonah. "I'm fascinated by your decision to become a mail-order preacher. I've never known anyone who did that."

Drew blinked. She knew Elise, and her sister didn't make idle chatter without a reason. Something about Jonah had snagged her attention.

"Hey, I like parties." Jonah smiled. "Now that I'm licensed to marry folks, I get to attend a whole bunch of parties."

Elise laughed. "Can't argue with that logic."

Now that Drew thought about it, she realized Elise had been more animated whenever the good-looking minister was around. Interesting. A crush on one of the members of the Thunder Mountain Brotherhood would be an excellent distraction from all the drama about the internship rejection that was going on in Billings.

Damon rejoined the group. "Ready to test the sound system."

"Good. Once I'm in position with my camera mic on, let 'er rip." Drew moved to the area of the barn she'd picked out for obtaining the best shots. She held up her hand. "Go!"

The first chords of the music chosen for the intro filled the space, surging into the rafters as if the structure had been transformed into a cathedral. The horses grew restless, stomping and nickering in protest.

"Tone it down!" Damon shouted.

The volume was reduced, but the horses still didn't like it. Their protest was more muted, but they were clearly not happy as they paced restlessly in their stalls. Drew suspected the ceremony would either include dramatic music or horses, but not both. Given time Cade, Lexi and Herb might have acclimated the animals to this, but they didn't have that kind of time.

After conferring with Cade, Lexi held up both hands. "Stop the music!" That got a laugh. She turned toward the two sound guys. "You have a magnificent system and without horses in here it would be spectacular. But Cade and I decided early on that the horses would be part of the ceremony, so that means the music won't work. We'd still like you to play for the reception. We'll pay you as if you did both. That's only fair."

"Thanks, ma'am," one of the men said. "Then we'll see you tomorrow afternoon." They began packing up their gear.

Next Lexi focused on Austin, who'd taken a seat on the end of one of the benches. "Jonah says you still play guitar."

He rose and stepped into the aisle. His six-three, muscular frame nearly filled it. "I do, but I'm not—"

"Austin, I'm asking you, I'm begging you, to play guitar for our wedding. For the intro you can play whatever you know, but if you can manage it, I'd love the traditional wedding march when I come in."

He tugged on his hat. "Turns out I know that tune."

"You do?"

"Had a couple who wanted to get married during a trail ride in New Zealand. They wanted that music so I learned it."

Lexi beamed at him. "You're a lifesaver."

"I wouldn't say that, ma'am."

"Well, I would. Could you fetch your guitar so we can continue with the rehearsal?"

"I can, but it needs a new set of strings. The sound won't be what I'd want it to be."

"It'll do for now," Lexi said. "Would you have time to get new strings before the ceremony?"

"I'll make time."

"Bless you, Austin Teague."

Drew looked on as Austin blushed, and her heart warmed in a way that could end up being very dangerous.

Elise nudged her in the ribs. "Gotcha, didn't he?"

"I didn't count on the guitar."

"Yeah, we never see those things coming until they hit us between the eyes."

"This doesn't change anything."

Elise chuckled. "Keep telling yourself that, sis."

After Austin returned with his guitar, the rehearsal went well, mostly because Jonah kept everyone on task. His sense of humor combined with his talent for managing a group of people made him perfect for the job. At one point Elise tapped Drew on the shoulder, pointed to Jonah and mouthed, *He's great.*

Drew nodded because she was also impressed. But she had trouble focusing on anyone other than the gorgeous cowboy playing his guitar. Maybe it needed new strings, but Austin compensated beautifully. After the rehearsal Lexi gave him a big hug and Drew would have loved to do the same. But she was working.

Although the wedding reception would take place in the rec hall near the cabins, Lexi and Cade had decided the rehearsal dinner should be around the fire pit, the favorite gathering spot for cookouts. Drew switched to a smaller camcorder so she could video the group walking down to the meadow. Several of the guests helped her out by peering into the lens and making faces during the short hike.

Elise carried Drew's camera bag and swapped jokes with everyone. As Drew had envisioned, her sister fit right in with the boisterous crowd, which was not unlike the Martinelli clan. Maybe that was why Austin's comment about seeing a lot of the family in the future had made her nervous. In her experience, family equaled turmoil and obligation.

Eventually she realized Jonah was keeping pace with them, too, and had started a conversation with Elise about Michelangelo. Whether he knew it or not, he'd found the surest way to her sister's heart. Drew was encouraged that he seemed as interested in Elise as she was in him.

Before Drew had started filming today she'd promised herself not to get more footage of Austin than of the bride and groom. Turned out it wouldn't be a problem because he never came within camera range. At the moment, he was up at the house helping a couple of his brothers bring the food and drinks down to the meadow. Not that she'd kept track of his whereabouts.

Yeah, right. She'd known right where that cowboy was at all times. She'd picked up on the conversation about who would haul down the dinner fixings and she'd heard Austin volunteer. He was keeping himself busy and that was a good thing because it left her free to do her work.

The setting and the upbeat mood of the guests made her job easy, too. In the waning light, she got some great shots of friends gathered by the fire against the rosy hues of sunset. Once the beer and champagne arrived, she recorded toasts and laughter, teasing and hugs.

Then, after the steaks were on the grill and everyone was gathered, Lexi and Cade produced two matching digital tablets loaded with the video Drew had created. Cade handed one to Rosie and Herb while Lexi handed the other to her folks, Janine and Aaron. The four of them chose to gather around one screen instead of turning on both.

As they started watching, Drew was afraid she'd lose it, but somehow she kept filming through her tears. By the time the video was over, the natural light was almost gone so she shut off her camera. Good thing, because she was suddenly besieged by Rosie, Herb, Janine and Aaron as they embraced her and poured out words of gratitude. Elise showed up to take her camera so it wouldn't hit the dirt.

The group hug ended with much wiping of eyes and blowing of noses. Several of the other guests were in the same shape and a slew of emotional toasts followed. When the entire group raised a glass to Drew, she was both choked up and humbled. One little video had brought so much joy.

Elise gave back the camera and wrapped an arm around her shoulders. "You did good, sis."

"Thank you." Drew sniffed and dug in her pocket for a tissue.

"Ever thought of making that your specialty?"

"Not really." She wiped her eyes. "I think the nature videos will be my specialty."

"Okay. Just thought I'd mention it." She looked past Drew's shoulder. "Hey, Austin. Didn't she do great?"

"She sure did."

Drew turned to find him walking toward her, wearing a broad smile. She'd last seen him tending the food on the grill, but then Cade and Lexi had brought out the video and she'd lost track of him. His sudden appearance delighted her and made her wish they could have a little alone time.

He gestured toward the camera. "I noticed you turned it off. Does that mean you're taking a break?"

"Actually I'm finished for the night. Cade and Lexi didn't want me to use artificial light during the cookout so they said when it got dark I should quit. I was about to take this one to my truck and get the other one out of the barn before the food's served." She hoped he'd get the hint.

"Then let me help you."

"Okay." She avoided looking directly at Elise as she retrieved the camera bag her sister was holding. One of them could easily start laughing. Having a sister who knew the score was both a curse and a blessing. "If anyone asks," she said to Elise, "tell them we'll be back soon."

"I will. Take your time." Her sister's voice trembled as if she might lose her cool any second.

Drew glanced at Austin. "Let's go."

He lengthened his stride to keep up with her. "In a hurry?"

"Yes. Wouldn't want the food to get cold." She tucked her camera in the bag and zipped it closed.

"God, no." And then he laughed softly.

His low, sexy chuckle was all it took to send her up in flames. She couldn't wait to get her hands on that cowboy.

Chapter Sixteen

Austin vibrated with the need to kiss Drew and hold her close, but he also didn't want to forget to say what he'd been thinking during the rehearsal and afterward. "Before we get to the barn and I forget everything but kissing you—"

"Oh, is that what we'll be doing?"

"Yes, ma'am, and I wish it could be more. But first let me say that you have an amazing gift. I thought so when I saw your dedication to filming the horses, and then tonight I was bowled over by your talent. I loved watching you work."

"Thank you."

"I heard Elise talk about making something your specialty. Did she mean weddings in general or the Lexi and Cade one?"

"I think she was talking about the one I made for them."

"Then I completely agree with her. Not everyone

would have the imagination or the talent for something like that. I only caught part of it, but judging from everyone's reaction, you nailed it."

"It was mostly their doing. They came across so authentically that all I had to do was capture the emotion they gave me."

"That's my point. Not everyone could. I know people have to be relaxed but they're bound to be because you're so warm and encouraging with them. I saw tonight how you make everyone feel at ease."

"That's easy, though."

"Again, not easy for everyone. You could expand that concept and offer thank-you videos from grandkids to their grandparents, or from a group of students to a teacher, or from employees to a wonderful boss."

"Except I want to concentrate on making the nature videos."

"Well, yeah, I know you do." For some reason, she was resisting the suggestion so he dropped it. "Just a thought. Did you want to get the camera out of the barn now or later?"

"Let's get it now."

"Works for me." He slid back the wooden bar holding the double doors closed and opened one side, his heart pounding. "After you."

She walked into the darkened interior and lowered her camera case to the floor. Then she turned back to him and stepped closer. "Is this what you had in mind, cowboy?"

"Yes, ma'am." His breath quickened. Dropping his hat on top of her camera bag, he pulled her close. "Exactly what I had in mind."

She wound her arms around his neck and snuggled against him. "You left me alone to do my work tonight. Thank you for that."

"Wasn't easy." He cradled the back of her head, splaying his fingers where she'd put her silky hair into a ponytail. "I love watching you work, but I kept thinking about doing this." Leaning down, he brushed his mouth over hers. "And especially this." He delved deep, moaning as he reconnected with the rich sensuality of kissing Drew.

And oh, how she kissed him back. The seductive way she welcomed the thrust of his tongue made him wish she hadn't been so against a long-term relationship. He could kiss her this way for the rest of their lives.

Lifting his mouth from hers, he gasped for breath. "I want you so much. If I thought we could…"

"We can't." She was breathing as fast as he was. "I want you, too, but…just…*kiss me.*" She pulled his head down, her mouth hot on his and her body so close he could feel the imprint of her pendant against his chest.

He hadn't dealt with frustration this intense since he'd been a virginal teenager who hadn't dared to take the next step.

Too soon, she backed away, panting. "We have to stop."

"I know." He ran a trembling hand through his hair. "I thought we could just kiss. Take the edge off."

She gulped. "Wrong."

"Get your other camera." He picked up his hat and her camera bag. "I'll wait by your truck."

"Never mind. I'll handle it. You can go back."

"No, ma'am." He dragged in another breath. "I walked you here and I'm walking you back."

"Because of cowboy manners?"

He couldn't tell if she was amused or irritated. "That and respect for Mom's rules. Guaranteed she noticed we left together. If I show up without you, I'll hear about it. I'll wait by the truck."

"I'll be there in a minute."

He stepped out into the cool night air and took a deep breath. He'd promised himself that he wouldn't go beyond a kiss and he'd damn near broken that promise. She deserved more than a quickie in the barn before they went back to the party. Drew was classier than that. Hell, *he* was classier than that.

Most of all, he didn't want to mess this thing up. Their conversation earlier today had alerted him that she wasn't ready to wear matching sweatshirts to the Thunder Mountain Christmas Eve gathering. She also wouldn't be inviting him to move in with her anytime soon.

Leaning against her truck, he evaluated where he was in this relationship. Not where he'd like to be, but not in a hopeless scenario, either. Unlike the lady in New Zealand, Drew liked his personality as well as his body. He could build on that.

"The truck's open." She showed up lugging the camera she'd mounted on a tripod. "If you'd get the door, I'd be—"

"Let me have that thing while you get the door." He lifted the camera away from her. "Where does it go?"

"Eventually it'll go in the back. I have a whole setup there for transporting my equipment but I didn't want to make this complicated. Elise can help me stow everything properly."

"Or we can do it the right way now." Shouldering her camera bag and carrying the heavy video camera, he walked to the back of the truck. "Tell me what goes where."

"Thanks, Austin." She put down the tailgate and showed him where to put the biggest camera.

"Happy to do it." He arranged everything in the bin and stood back so she could close the tailgate. "Now let's get going because I'm developing a strong urge to kiss you again." He took her hand and started off. Then he gave her hand a squeeze. "Is this okay?"

"If your family operates anything like mine, everybody knows about our camping trip by now, so it's not like we're fooling anybody."

"No, we're not. But I thought you didn't want to give people the wrong impression about…about where we stand."

She pulled him to a stop. "I'll admit I used to care what other people thought about my love life, but that's a waste of time."

"I agree."

"But you and I have to be clear with each other. Are we?"

"Yes, ma'am. Totally clear." And he was determined to be patient and wait for her to realize they were perfect together. Then again, a woman who kissed the way Drew did might have a change of heart sooner rather than later.

"Then you're welcome to hold my hand for as long as you like."

"Okay, I will." He didn't add that if he had his way, he'd be holding her hand for the next fifty or sixty years.

"Are you planning to bring your guitar back out tonight?"

"God, no. I managed to stumble through the rehearsal, but I'm not pushing my luck. By wedding kickoff time, I'll have a new set of strings on that baby."

"I should mic it to make sure we can hear it during the video."

"I'm cool with that. But give me until noon to find the strings and tune it."

"I'll be here for most of the day."

"Most of the day? But the ceremony isn't until five."

"I know, but there are lots of important things to film before then. I want to video the arranging of the flowers in the barn and the little girl braiding the horses' manes. Then I need to document the separation of the guys and gals, which is always tricky in a situation like this."

"The women will get the house and the men will get the cabins in the meadow. Except for Herb. I'm guessing he might be a floater between the two camps."

"I'll be a floater, too. After I film the ladies getting dressed I might head down to the meadow and see how many of the guys will let me show them getting duded up in their outfits."

"I don't know. That's sacred ground, brotherhood only."

"I understand. I don't want to be obnoxious about it, but years from now you might all want some candid shots of adjusting each other's string ties and pulling on your fancy dress boots."

"We might. Listen, I should tell you that when I play the wedding march, the brotherhood has talked about humming it along with the guitar."

"Austin, I love that. Gives me cold chills."

"No promises. Not everyone is in favor."

"Talk them into it. I think it would be awesome."

"We haven't told Cade or Lexi."

"Yeah, well, don't. Then you have the option of doing it or not depending how everyone feels at the time. But you have my vote. This wedding is so nontraditional that whatever you decide to do will be fine. I'll just go with it."

Austin squeezed her hand. "That's what I'm talking about. You have a great way of rolling with the punches.

I'm learning from you that good footage of people has to be spontaneous and you've got that part down. I know your heart's set on the nature videos, but—" He caught himself. "Never mind." He was doing it again, pushing for a scenario that she hadn't been enthusiastic about. His motives weren't pure, either, since he favored a plan that wouldn't require so much travel.

"What were you going to say?"

"I was sticking my nose in again where it doesn't belong. This is your career."

"That's true but you're allowed to give an opinion."

"Not when I have ulterior motives."

They were within sight of the group gathered around the fire pit but she pulled him to a stop again. "I wondered about that."

He decided not to waffle on the issue. "You need to follow your heart, like your grandmother said, and if that means traveling south during the winter months, I'll accept that and be happy for you. We have no ties to each other." He looked into her eyes. "And I'll miss you like crazy whenever you're gone."

Her gaze warmed as she studied him. "If I'm totally honest, I'd miss you, too. But that's not a reason to ditch the idea."

"Definitely not." Although he sure liked hearing that she'd miss him and he *really* liked the way she was looking at him. Maybe she'd miss him enough to invite him along once in a while, assuming he could afford the time and expense. But he wouldn't ask her. Like his brothers had said, she needed to do the asking.

He gave her hand a squeeze. "I just hope you won't reject the thank-you video concept entirely. I saw your face when those folks were watching what you'd created.

You captured something precious and I could tell what it meant to you."

Her expression softened. "It did mean a lot."

"Then that's all I'll say on the subject. Let's go grab some food."

Chapter Seventeen

Drew and Austin each got a plate of food and Damon handed them glasses of champagne. "Word is that we have some announcements coming up and you'll need these for toasting," he said.

"Then we'd better find a bench and sit." Austin glanced around.

"Over here, guys." Elise beckoned from where she sat with Jonah. "We saved you a spot."

Drew noted the space between her sister and Jonah on the bench, or rather the lack of it. There would be plenty of room for two more. "Thanks, sis." She walked over and settled down next to Elise, who'd finished most of her meal.

Austin took a seat next to her and leaned around her to smile at Elise and Jonah. "Appreciate it, folks."

Jonah smiled. "No worries. We knew you'd be along eventually."

Drew balanced her plate on her lap. "Were we missed?"

"A few people asked. I told them you were putting away your equipment and double-checking all the electrical connections." She looked over at Drew and blinked innocently. "Did you take care of that?"

"Yes. Yes, I did. Everything's fine." She returned her sister's bland expression. "Listen, I've been thinking about tomorrow. I'll need to be here all day, but you probably don't want to hang out here that long."

"I won't mind a bit. It'll be fun to see everything take shape. I've never spent much time on a ranch. Rosie thinks I should mosey on down here every couple of weeks, but I told her you'd probably get sick of me if I visited that often."

"I would not. I'd love having you."

"I've offered to teach her to ride," Jonah said.

"And I'd really like that." Elise's expression grew animated as she turned to Drew. "You should learn, too. Remember how we used to talk about it and never did?"

"You don't know how to ride?" Austin's eyebrows lifted.

"Too busy doing other sports, I guess."

"So when you offered to shoot my first trail ride, were you just going to climb on a horse without ever having done it?"

She laughed. "Guess I hadn't thought that through. I'm fairly coordinated so I figured I'd catch on pretty quick, but maybe I could use a few lessons so I don't fall off in the middle of filming."

"And you might want to consider logging time in the saddle before you tackle an overnight trip." Austin looked amused. "You have to work up to spending several hours on a horse or you'll be miserable."

"The four of us could go out," Jonah said. "And we

need to do it before the first snow. Let's pick a weekend and—"

"Attention everybody!" Cade tapped a fork against his champagne flute. "Ty and Whitney have an announce—"

"Oh, my God!" Rosie charged over to throw her arms around both of them, knocking Ty's hat off in the process. He didn't seem to notice as he gathered his wife and his foster mom in a tight embrace.

"Boy or girl?" someone called out.

"You'll all have to wait another six months to find out!" Whitney beamed as everyone crowded around with congratulations.

When Austin and Jonah rose to their feet, Drew put down her plate and stood, too. She didn't know Ty and Whitney well, but she'd be happy to add her good wishes to the mix.

"Hold on, hold on!" Cade tapped his glass again. "Hope and Liam also have an—" He wasn't allowed to finish that sentence, either, before pandemonium erupted a second time.

"And we're having a girl!" Liam's deep baritone carried over the noise of the crowd.

His jubilant expression tickled Drew. Such a caring, positive man would make a great dad.

Cade tapped on his glass a third time.

"Another one?" Rosie's face was flushed with excitement as she surveyed the crowd.

"I don't think so, Mom," Cade said, "but I wanted to check before we made the toast. Anybody else have news to share?"

"Not yet, bro." Finn, the brewer from Seattle, wrapped an arm around his wife, Chelsea. "But we're working on it!"

That got a laugh and Cade's nod of approval. "That's

great to hear. Can't have too many grandbabies, right, Mom?"

"Never!" Rosie's eyes sparkled in the light from the fire. "Bring on those Thunder Mountain babies!"

Drew fingered her pendant. Her grandmother had been surrounded by what Drew considered a daunting number of children and grandchildren. But that was a fraction of what Rosie could be looking at in a few years. She seemed ecstatic about it. The image made Drew shiver.

"Cold?" Austin slipped an arm around her shoulders.

"Not really. I just thought about how many little kids Rosie could have running around here before too long."

Austin chuckled. "And she can't wait."

"I noticed that."

"The woman's incredible. I sometimes think not having kids of her own was how it was supposed to be. She turned into a kind of superhero mom. All she's missing is the cape." He gave Drew a squeeze. "Come on. Let's go over and congratulate the happy parents."

She did that, and she was genuinely happy for them because they seemed so delighted with the concept themselves. As she listened politely to a discussion of prenatal vitamins and morning sickness, car seats and portable cribs, she was so grateful that she wasn't standing in either one of those wives' shoes. Having a Thunder Mountain baby was a great big flipping deal, a goal she couldn't imagine having.

She couldn't say the same for Austin, though. He was clearly in the swing of this new stage in the life of Thunder Mountain Ranch. He asked more questions than anybody, or so it seemed to her. If she didn't know better, she'd think he'd already lined up his baby mama.

Maybe he had. He'd said all the right words about having fun without any strings or promises, but judging from his intense interest in the baby news, he was eager to start a family. She was not. By continuing their affair, she was selfishly wasting his valuable time.

The party lasted a little longer after that, but everyone agreed that they all needed to get some rest before the big day.

Before they left, Cade asked for everyone's attention one last time. "I got a special phone call today. My cousin Jack Chance and his mom, my aunt Sarah, are driving over from Jackson Hole tomorrow."

Drew blinked. The reputation of the Chance brothers, co-owners of the Last Chance Ranch, had spread as far as Billings. She vaguely remembered serving one of the brothers at Martinelli's during her waitressing days. It might have been Jack.

"Oh, Cade." Lexi looked at him with shining eyes. "That's fantastic. When were you going to tell me?"

"Couldn't decide the right moment. Didn't want to interfere with the baby news, so this seemed like the perfect time." He glanced around at the group. "Some of you know the story and some don't, but two years ago I didn't think I had any blood relatives. Finding out I was related to the owners of the Last Chance Ranch came as a big shock."

"But you've adjusted, right, bro?" Finn smiled. "Sure seems like it."

"I have, and I feel like a lucky son of a gun to have them as relatives. We invited the whole family, although God knows where we would have put them all considering our limited seating. They couldn't bring everyone because of schedule conflicts, so Jack and Aunt Sarah are representing the family."

"I can't wait to meet them." Rosie gave Cade a hug. "This is wonderful news, son."

"It'll be good to see them again," Finn said. "Chels and I got to spend a few days at the Last Chance two years ago. We'd be glad to introduce them around."

Chelsea laughed. "From what I remember of Jack Chance, he'll need no introduction. The guy's a force of nature."

Yep, Drew decided. She'd served Jack Chance. Martinelli's piped in music from a sound system but they had no dance floor. Jack had insisted on dancing her around the tables anyway when one of his favorite songs had come on. Then he'd left her a huge tip.

"So is that it for startling announcements?" Damon lifted a sleeping Sophie from Phil's arms. "Because I need to get my ladies tucked in for the night."

"And I need my beauty sleep." Lexi gave Cade a quick kiss. "See you at the altar, cowboy."

Cade stared at her. "You're really going home with your parents? I thought you were kidding."

"Not kidding."

"But I'll be all by myself."

"You'll have your cat." She gave him another kiss, this time on the cheek. "Bye, sweetie."

"Damn." Cade looked crestfallen. "Ringo's great, but he doesn't say much."

Austin glanced at Drew. "I'll walk you to your truck, but I need to talk with Cade first. Wait for me?"

"Sure."

"Jonah and I will go on ahead," Elise said. "The truck's unlocked, right?"

"Yep."

"We'll probably take our time. It's a gorgeous night."

"That it is." Jonah slipped his hand through hers as they left the meadow.

Drew took comfort in her sister's enjoyment of this

flirtation with Jonah. It might turn into something or fizzle out, but for now Elise seemed to have forgotten about Italy.

Austin had his arm around Cade's shoulders as they talked. She didn't want to eavesdrop so she moved a little farther away. Snippets still drifted in her direction, though—things like "important day," "fancy dress" and "Lexi's special moment." She concluded that Austin had given plenty of thought to the subject of brides and weddings, too.

His conversation with Cade had obviously cheered up the bridegroom because now he and Austin were laughing like fools. Finn and Ty walked over to get in on whatever it was while Chelsea and Whitney stood together watching and shaking their heads.

"See you jokers later," Austin said as he left the group and started toward Drew.

"Don't do anything I wouldn't do, Junior," Cade called after him.

Finn laughed. "That leaves a hell of a lot of territory!" He added something else that Drew couldn't hear and the guys launched into another fit of laughter.

Austin came toward her grinning. "Mission accomplished. Couldn't stand to see that sad look on his face."

"I know. I realize there's a tradition that the bride isn't supposed to see the groom the morning of the wedding, but when they've been living together isn't that sort of pointless?"

"I think this is about Lexi's bond with her parents. She wants one more chance to go home and be their little girl again."

"Oh." She was touched by his insight. "Then it makes perfect sense. She loves them a lot. That was clear from the way she thanked them in the video. But it does leave Cade alone with his cat."

"He won't be." Austin took her hand and wove his fingers through hers as they started toward the barn. "Since Jonah and I are the unattached ones, we'll spend the night up at his cabin. I suggested it and he liked the idea. I'm sure Jonah will go along with it, too. We'll drink some beer, play some cards."

"That's very nice of you." Holding hands with Austin was a pleasure she was growing increasingly fond of. As they walked she savored the warmth, strength and affection he communicated with that simple gesture. If she ultimately decided to give up that pleasure, that would be a sad day.

"Hey, we're brothers. It's what we do for each other."

"But you'll also get some sleep, right?"

"Worried about me?"

"I am, but I'm even more concerned about Cade from a practical standpoint. If he's dead on his feet and he's the only one with the mic, then the ceremony could suck, which would be disappointing for everyone."

"Tell you what. I'll make it my job to see that he gets some shut-eye tonight. How's that?"

"Helpful. Thank you."

"I noticed your sister and Jonah went ahead of us. That could mean they want to be alone for a while."

"I'm guessing they do."

"Then we should meander along and give them some extra time." He slowed his pace. "Come to think of it, they might be to the kissing stage by now."

"They might."

"Speaking of kissing..."

And here she was, yearning to feel his strong arms

around her and yet wondering if she would only create heartache in the long run.

He didn't seem to notice her hesitation. "The minute I took your hand my brain checked out. It's a wonder I managed that much of a segue."

"I thought it was cute." His use of the word *segue* reminded her of another quality she admired about him. He was literate, and not in a stuffy, self-important way. He'd read books because he'd loved the stories.

He squeezed her hand. "Here's my idea. There's a place in the shadows beside the barn. If we slide into that spot before we get to your truck, Jonah and Elise won't even know we're there."

"I see." She tried to summon the willpower to refuse. She failed.

"I really need to kiss you again before you leave tonight."

Heat suffused her body and she resisted the urge to fan herself. "We should probably discuss something else."

"Like what?"

"Tell me about Jonah."

"Ah, okay. Let me recalibrate some brain cells. Jonah. Somewhat footloose. Man of a million ideas who can't settle on any one of them for long. Drove me crazy until I accepted that he might drift from one thing to another for the rest of his life."

"You don't think being a licensed minister will turn into anything?"

"No, ma'am. He enjoys marrying folks but said he can't settle on one denomination. Most churches expect you to declare a preference."

"True."

"He's good with people and horses. Dude ranch work suits him. Is that enough about Jonah?"

"Is he nice to women?"

"Always. But picky. He must think your sister is special since he's taken an interest."

"She is special. Someday she'll be living in a large city because that's where she'll find the right job. Jonah doesn't seem like a big-city kind of guy."

"He's not."

"But if he's the footloose type…"

"Exactly. They can have some temporary fun." He pulled her to a stop and smiled down at her. "I don't think you have to worry, Drew. He's a good guy. And I'd love to change the subject."

Her pulse kicked into high gear. "Okay."

"Come with me, pretty lady." He led her to their right, avoiding the pool of light cast by the dusk-to-dawn lamp mounted over the barn doors. Then he hung his hat on the end of the hitching post.

They ended up in deep shadow on the side of the barn farthest away from where her truck was parked. She kept her voice down. "Was that hat some kind of signal?"

"Used to be. Don't know if anybody remembers." He pulled her close.

"I can barely see you."

"You don't need to see me." He cradled her jaw in one hand and pressed his thumb to the corner of her mouth. "Just let me in."

She instinctively parted her lips and he was there, the firm pressure of his lips coaxing her to open even more. With a soft groan, he thrust his tongue inside. Then he proceeded to hold her head very still as he ravished her mouth. He took possession of every inch, teasing, nipping and using his tongue in ways that made her writhe against him in frustration.

Shoving her hands in his back pockets, she pressed

her hips tight against his groin and yearned for the barriers between them to magically disappear. He pushed her against the side of the barn and nestled his aroused package between her parted thighs.

Slowly he raised his head. His voice was strained. "Let the record show that I really want you right now." He gulped for air. "But I'm going to control myself."

She took a shaky breath. "Am I supposed to be thankful?"

"I sure hope not." He nudged the aching spot between her thighs. "I hope you're thinking about when we can solve our mutual problem."

"Sunday night." They had issues, but they needed time and privacy to sort them out.

"That's an eternity from now."

"I know."

"But we'll make it." He shuddered. "Not sure how, but…" He sighed. "We will." Touching his mouth very lightly to hers, he gently sucked on her lower lip.

She was definitely wound too tight, because that simple caress nearly sent her over the edge.

Slowly he backed away. "No more." He sucked in air. "No more good-night kisses."

"Just…just as well."

"I'm holding out for a good-morning one."

"Not tomorrow, though. I'll be—"

"I'm not talking about tomorrow."

"Oh."

"When you come back from Billings on Sunday, I want the whole night."

She swallowed. "Okay."

"Good. That's settled." He took a deep breath. "Excuse me while I do a little pacing. I need to walk off some of this tension."

"I understand."

He chuckled. "I doubt that, but thanks for the support." He winced. "Once you're in the truck and on your way, I'll be much better."

"I don't want to startle Jonah and my sister. How did you want to work this?"

"We'll approach the truck while having an animated conversation."

"Not necessary, bro." Jonah came around the corner of the barn carrying Austin's hat. "I left Elise sitting in the truck. Then I saw this and figured I'd hang out by the hitching post until I heard what sounded like normal conversation."

"So you did remember."

"Sort of. I recognized your hat and you were wearing it when Elise and I left the meadow, so if it was now on the hitching post that logically had to be a make-out signal."

Drew pushed away from the side of the barn. "If Elise is ready to go, then I'd better get over there."

"No rush," Jonah said. "She thought you two might linger along the way."

"That's what comes from double-dating with my sister. She knows way too much."

Austin came toward her. "I'll walk you over there."

"Tell you what." She reached up and touched his cheek where his whiskers were starting to grow. "You and Jonah can stand by the barn and watch to make sure I get in the truck and drive away without incident. But you really don't need to escort me over there."

"She's right," Jonah said.

"But—"

"I know that isn't how Rosie taught us, but there are times you need to throw out the rule book."

Austin laughed. "Do you even have a rule book anymore? You've been throwing it out ever since I knew you."

"I have one. It just doesn't look like everyone else's."

Drew filed that comment away. She might need to pay closer attention to this budding relationship and make sure her sister didn't get hurt by some cowboy with a different set of principles. "So is the consensus that I can walk to the truck on my own?"

"Yes, ma'am." Austin glanced at Jonah. "I'm overruled."

"Then I'll leave you both. Have fun keeping Cade company while he waits for his wedding day. Good night." She gave Austin a quick kiss on the cheek and walked away.

When she climbed into the cab, Elise glanced over at her. "I have a crush on that cowboy."

"Tell me something I don't already know." She fished the keys out from under the seat and started the truck. "FYI, according to Austin, Jonah's not the type to live in a big city."

"I figured that out. Who knows? Maybe I'm not, either."

"What are you talking about? All you've ever wanted was a job curating an extensive art collection for a major museum. You're not going to find that job in a small town."

"I know, but losing this internship has made me reevaluate."

"That's fine, but please don't let a good-looking cowboy, who, by the way, has no idea what he wants from life, derail your entire career plan."

"He knows what he wants."

"Like what? I mean aside from the obvious short-term goal that we don't need to lay out in detail."

"He wants a life based on meaning instead of material possessions. I find that sexy."

"Material possessions like fine art?"

"We didn't get into that, but he gave me something to think about—fine art as stuff. It's a concept I hadn't considered before."

Drew groaned. "I'm not liking the sound of this."

"I didn't think you would. But it's not like we're in love or anything so you can stand down, sis."

"Yeah, okay. I'll admit it's a hot-button issue for me so I'm probably overreacting, or projecting, or whatever the terms are."

"I'd believe that. So how are things going with Austin? You didn't look terribly excited during all the talk about babies."

"I'm totally happy for those couples if that's what they want. But that's not where I am in my life. I'm becoming convinced that's where Austin's at, though."

"Honestly, that wouldn't surprise me. You said he's been with Rosie and Herb since he was nine and Rosie loves weddings and kids. I picked up on that immediately."

"So you think I might be right that he's ready to start a family of his own?" She glanced over at Elise. "Even though he says we can just hang out and have fun?"

"Considering his behavior tonight, maybe he is ready to settle down, despite what he's said to you. You have more info to go on now. I'd suggest another heart-to-heart with the man."

Drew sighed. "I'll do that. But the wedding doesn't make that kind of conversation easy. Then again, if it hadn't been for the wedding, he might not have come back from New Zealand when he did."

"Do you regret meeting him?"

She thought about it. "No. I'll never regret meeting Austin. He's one of the good guys." She took a deep breath. "But that doesn't mean we're meant for each other."

Chapter Eighteen

By Saturday morning Austin could see that Cade was a nervous wreck. Playing cards and drinking beer was no longer an appropriate distraction. Since Austin needed a trip to town for guitar strings, he proposed Jonah and Cade go with him. They could fuel up with breakfast at the diner, pick up the strings and shop for some decorative doodads to make the cabin more festive when Lexi returned that night.

Two hours later they arrived back at the cabin with the new strings plus a boatload of scented candles, flower arrangements, various types of chocolates, wine and a teddy bear couple dressed in wedding outfits. The bears had been Austin's idea.

"I'm doing this when I get married," he said as he surveyed the stash on the kitchen table and the kitchen counters. "What a great idea to welcome her with all these goodies."

Cade rubbed the back of his neck. "Hope so."

"If nothing else, she'll be touched by knowing you wanted to do something special." Jonah nudged back his hat. "And you won't have to find a place for anything except the bears. It's not like we've added a bunch of things you'll have to dust."

"That's a good point," Cade said. "I used to think Mom didn't have knickknacks because we'd break them. Recently she told me it was the dust factor."

Austin picked up the two bears. "You don't have to dust these, either. Just whack them together, like this." He gave a quick demonstration.

"Hey!" Cade snatched them away from him. "Don't do that."

"Why not? It's a great dusting technique."

"That may be true, but Cade Bear and Lexi Bear would prefer to have the dust carefully brushed from their furry little bodies." Cade walked over and gently placed them side by side on the sofa. "They don't appreciate being smashed together like a pair of cymbals."

Jonah was cracking up. "*Cade Bear and Lexi Bear*? Are you really gonna call them that?"

"Sure, why not?"

"Because it's not manly. It sounds like you're three."

"No, it doesn't." Since Austin had insisted on the bears he felt the need to defend Cade. "What else would you call them? They're supposed to represent the happy couple. You can't name them George and Sheila."

"Why do you have to name them at all?"

"Because that's what you do with stuffed animals. I had a bear I called Teddy. Not very original but I came up with it when I was around two, according to what my mom told me."

Cade nodded. "I had a bear. Named him Rufus after the character on *Sesame Street*. When I thought I was too old for teddy bears, I gave him to a younger kid."

"Yeah, I did that, too. When my mom died, I wished I had him back, but it was too late. That little kid was attached to Teddy and I didn't have the heart."

Jonah gazed at them. "Well, I didn't have a bear, so I guess that explains it."

"Doesn't have to be a bear," Austin said. "Like you heard last night, Sophie has a plush tarantula. I knew a kid who had a plush snake."

"Well, I didn't have any of those critters. Didn't know there was a naming protocol involved."

Austin couldn't believe that he'd lived in the same cabin with Jonah for years and hadn't known the guy had never had a stuffed toy as a kid. No telling what else Jonah had done without, but it might explain his philosophy about material possessions. He exchanged a quick glance with Cade.

"You know what?" Cade gestured toward the items piled in the kitchen. "We're standing here shooting the breeze like we have all day and we don't. I want to spit shine this cabin before we start putting flowers and candles everywhere and the morning is slip-sliding away."

"That's the damned truth." Jonah seemed relieved for a change of topic. "When are these long-lost relatives of yours going to show up, by the way?"

"They said not to expect them until right before the ceremony. They're checking into a hotel in town because they know we're full up here. If you're asking whether I should be down at the house soon in case they arrive, the answer is no. We need to start the cleaning project ASAP, though."

"I'll help you with that." Jonah jerked a thumb at Austin. "John Denver has to restring his guitar and practice his tunes."

"Yeah, I do."

"Then take that project out to the porch, please," Cade said, "so we don't have to vacuum around you."

"Do you want to vet the songs? Yesterday I was just winging it but you can have different ones as long as I know them."

"What you played yesterday was fine. I trust your judgment. Just don't play stuff like 'Does My Ring Burn Your Finger' or 'Whose Bed Have Your Boots Been Under?' and we'll be good."

"Damn. You just nixed my two favorites."

Cade grinned at him. "Grab your guitar and get outta here, cowboy. And thanks. It'll be great having you play."

"Especially when I launch into 'All My Ex's Live in Texas.' I know you want that one."

"There's the door, Junior."

Austin chuckled as he picked up the box of strings from the kitchen table and grabbed his guitar from the corner of the living room. He also took his phone out to the porch and laid it on the railing so he'd hear it. The men and women staying at the ranch were supposed to remain mostly separated today, but he remembered that Drew wanted to mic his guitar.

They couldn't be testing the mic at the last minute, either. If she didn't contact him by midafternoon, he'd text her. This was important, but it was also a great excuse to see her and maybe steal another kiss or two. He was getting seriously addicted to those kisses.

An hour later he had the guitar tuned and had started through his memorized pieces. None of them were sad songs or even mad songs. He'd never cared for those and Cade knew it.

Sitting on Cade's porch on a sunny day with his guitar balanced on his thigh was almost perfect. A light breeze was blowing and the birds were chirping away. Having Drew in the chair next to him would complete the picture but they were a long way from an idyllic scene like that. Neither one of them had a porch, for one thing.

He'd planned to rent an apartment but now he was thinking a house would be better, a small house with a porch. Porches and guitars were a natural fit. He might be able to find something like that at a rental price he could afford.

Staying overnight in Cade's house had given him a clearer picture of what he eventually wanted, although the place was a little small if Cade and Lexi had kids. He wondered if they'd thought of that. He sure would when he bought or built a house.

The door opened and Cade and Jonah came out with a big bag of chips and three beers. Cade handed Austin one of the beers and leaned against the porch railing while Jonah took the other chair. "This is lunch," Cade said. "We figured after a big breakfast we could survive on a snack until dinner."

"Works for me." Austin put down his guitar and twisted the cap off his beer. "You finished in there?"

"Yep." Jonah ripped open the bag of chips. "We came out here so we won't drop chips on the floor, although it's so clean you could eat off it."

"Am I allowed to walk on it?"

"Only if you take off your boots," Jonah said. "And don't touch anything."

"What'd you do with my duffel?"

"It's sitting by the front door along with mine. My recommendation is we finish our beer, grab our stuff and head down to the meadow so we don't mess up anything in the house. We have to go down there eventually to get dressed, and we can shower and shave in the bathhouse."

Austin smiled. "Like old times."

"Exactly." Jonah sipped his beer. "No telling how often a bunch of us will be together so we might as well make the most of it."

Austin grabbed a handful of chips. "We'll be doing this again before you know it. I'll be inviting the whole crew to my wedding."

Cade choked on his beer.

"Okay, okay. I don't have a date set or anything, but—"

"Or a *bride*." Cade looked at him and shook his head. "Please learn from my mistakes. You rush this thing and you'll live to regret it."

"It all turned out okay for you in the end, though. You're marrying Lexi and you have this great cabin."

"This extremely clean and tastefully appointed cabin," Jonah said.

"You're right, Junior. I have this cabin and a wonderful woman to share it with. But it's taken two very long years to get to this day because I tried to rush the process in the beginning. I'm trying to save you from screwing up like I did." He reached for some chips and dropped crumbs on the porch. "Whoops."

"No worries," Jonah said. "I parked the broom next to the door so we can sweep down the porch before we leave." Then he turned to Austin. "Cade's right. There's no doubt she likes you, but I wouldn't try to sell her on the wedding gig just yet."

Austin sighed and glanced around. "It's just that I know what I want now. I want her and a house, something like this. I'm already twenty-six, and—"

"You're *only* twenty-six," Cade said.

"My dad was thirty-two when he died." He didn't

bring that up often but it might be the only way his brothers would understand.

Cade's quick glance of solidarity showed that he did. "My mom was thirty-five. I get what you're saying. But I guarantee Drew isn't coming from that same place."

"Most people aren't," Jonah said. "And while it's good to know that time is precious, you can't railroad folks."

"Like a bullet train," Cade said with a grin.

Austin rolled his eyes.

"Well, he said *railroad*. You can't expect me to pass that up."

"Obviously." Austin took a long swallow of his beer and rested the bottle on his knee as he gazed at his brothers. "Well, it turns out you're both right. She asked me out for coffee yesterday to find out whether I was thinking long-term commitment already. I didn't mention that conversation last night because I didn't want to hear either of you say 'I told you so.'"

Cade grimaced. "Knowing me, I would have said it."

"Not me." Jonah polished off his beer. "I'd rather say it now when we're all sober. Hey, brother, I told you so!"

Austin threw a chip at him.

"No food fights allowed!" Jonah carefully picked the chip from the porch floor and tossed it into the yard for the birds. "I'll get the broom and both duffel bags if you two losers want to head for my truck."

Austin drank the last of his beer. "What about the bottles?"

"We're taking them and the bag of chips," Jonah said. "When we leave, there will be no trace of us anywhere."

"Except for the candy, the flowers, the candles and the teddy bears." Austin stood. "I'll get my own duffel. I want to take a peek inside."

"Yeah, okay." Jonah opened the door and pulled out the broom. "We did an awesome job if I do say so."

Austin grabbed his duffel and set it on the porch. Then he surveyed the house, or as much of it as he could see from the open doorway. Flower arrangements, bowls of candy and candles in various sizes sat on the coffee table, the mantel and the kitchen table. The two bears on the sofa added the perfect touch and he was glad he'd insisted on them.

"You need to move," Jonah said. "I want to sweep."

"Hang on." Austin went back and picked up his phone from the porch railing. "I want a picture."

"Don't show it to anybody," Cade said. "I want Lexi to be surprised."

"I won't. This is for me, so I can remember what we did." He took several shots. "I wish now I'd bought another set of those bears. You don't find those everywhere."

Jonah clapped him on the shoulder. "I'll make you a promise, bro. When it's your turn, I'll scour the internet for those bears."

"Okay. Thanks." But Austin didn't trust doing it that way. Some things you needed to hold in your hands to make sure they were right. In the next few days he'd go into town and buy another pair of the stuffed toys. It couldn't hurt to have them on hand.

He was still holding his phone when the text came in from Drew. When can U stop by the barn? Need 2 mic your guitar. His world suddenly became several shades brighter. He texted her back to say he'd be there in five minutes.

"What a big smile you're wearing, Junior," Cade said. "Can I guess who that text was from?"

"She needs me to come to the barn so she can mic my guitar."

Jonah laughed. "That's a new one. I've heard *clean the windows* and *mow the lawn*, but not *mic my guitar.*"

"She really does need to."

"I know. Just needling you. Would you like us to drop you off at the barn?"

"I would." He rode in the back of Jonah's truck on the way down and had to keep a firm grip on his hat and his guitar because the ride was breezy and bumpy. It suited his upbeat mood perfectly. He'd get to see Drew again, and with any luck, she'd be alone.

Chapter Nineteen

Drew had picked up sound equipment before driving to the ranch this morning. She'd also brought a wooden stool from her kitchen because Austin would need something to sit on and he might not have thought of that.

Elise was up at the house shooting video with Drew's small camera as the women fixed each other's hair and steamed the wrinkles out of their dresses. Drew liked to include that footage in the final cut, so it was a good thing she had help handling it while she was down in the barn trying to figure out the best spot to put Austin. The music setup was critical and until that was done to her satisfaction she wouldn't breathe easy.

When Austin walked in carrying his guitar, her pulse jumped the way it always did when she saw him. But she was determined to keep their interaction businesslike. She'd thought about him quite a bit today and she'd always come back to the same sad conclusion—his vision of the future was very different from hers.

"Howdy, ma'am." He leaned his guitar in the corner and hung his hat on it before coming toward her wearing that killer smile.

"Did you actually just say 'howdy, ma'am'?"

"I did. I like saying it. Makes me think of the olden days." With no hesitation whatsoever, he drew her into his arms. "I was hoping you'd be all by yourself."

"Elise is taking footage up at the house." Keeping their interaction businesslike wasn't quite so simple when he was used to kissing her whenever they were alone.

"Good." He pulled her close.

"And we have work to do." Somehow she'd ended up with her palms flattened against his broad chest. His heart was beating as fast as hers. "This probably isn't a good idea."

"I think it's a great idea." He cupped the back of her head and leaned closer. "I won't be able to concentrate unless I kiss you first." He captured her mouth.

Kissing him had always made the world disappear, but not this time. All that thinking about their situation had her on edge.

Slowly he lifted his head and gazed down at her. "Drew, what's wrong?"

"I'm just… We need to talk, but there's no time for it now."

His breath hitched. "You're right about that, but we'll have time tomorrow night."

"Yes, we will."

Slowly he released her and stepped back. "Do you still want me to come by?"

She hated seeing the uncertainty in his gaze, but this would be a terrible time to discuss whether they should consider parting ways.

"Yes, please." She put a hand to her chest and struggled to breathe normally. "But I could be late."

"I don't care what time it is. I hope you'll call me regardless."

"Okay."

He massaged the back of his neck and stared at her. "You wore your hair down."

"I didn't want to be quite so casual today. I'll be changing clothes in a little while, too." She took a deep breath. "If you'll get your guitar, we can see if this microphone placement works."

He didn't move. "When you wear your hair down, it curls more. I didn't realize that. I love the way it looks."

"Thank you. But we really need to—"

"Get down to business. I know. It's just that…you're beautiful."

She looked into his eyes and saw everything she'd been afraid he was feeling reflected there. She wasn't wrong about his intentions. The two of them were a train wreck in the making. Pain sliced through her when she thought of how that could hurt him.

He cleared his throat. "Just couldn't go without saying that." He gestured toward the mic. "Ready to test that thing out?"

She nodded.

"I'll get my guitar."

Moments later, she adjusted the sound levels and the position of the mic while Austin played country love songs. He didn't sing the lyrics but it didn't matter because she knew most of them. She also knew he was playing those songs for her.

Concentrating on the sound quality was a challenge when she kept thinking of how he'd looked at her. What a mess. Watching him play tore her into little pieces because he was obviously serenading her. A sweet serenade was the last thing she deserved now that it seemed certain she would break his heart.

"That's probably enough," she said. "I'm satisfied if you are."

He slid off the stool. "The mic's good and I like the acoustics in this old barn. Didn't know if I would. Now if you'll excuse me, I'll head on down to the meadow so I can spruce up for the big event." At the door he turned back. "Listen, whatever it is, we'll work it out. See you later."

When he was gone, she sank down on one of the benches to catch her breath. She was still there trying to sort through her volatile emotions when Elise came back.

Her sister hurried over, sat beside her and wrapped an arm around her shoulders. "What happened?"

"Austin's in love with me."

"He said that?"

"No, but I can see it in his eyes. And he thinks we can work out our differences but I don't think we can. We're on completely different trajectories." She sighed.

"Is there anything I can do?"

Drew shook her head. "Thanks for the offer, though."

"Are you absolutely sure you're not in love with him?"

"I'm not sure at all. The way this hurts right now, I very well might be. But if I do love him, the kindest thing would be to let him go. I have a gut feeling that he wants marriage and babies and I think he wants them soon."

"You haven't asked him, though."

"Not yet. Now isn't a great time to discuss it. But I will, probably after I drive back tomorrow night."

Elise nodded. "That sounds like a reasonable plan." She squeezed Drew's shoulder. "If I know you, and I think I do, you'll feel better once you get back to work."

"True."

"The women are about to put on their finery, which probably means the men will be doing that, too. You wanted one of us in each locker room, as I recall. Which are you taking?"

She didn't even have to think twice. "The women."

"All things considered, excellent choice. I'm not in love with Jonah so I'll have a steadier hand on the camcorder."

"Don't fall in love with him."

Elise smiled. "I can't promise you that, sis. He's pretty cute." She stood. "You have another one of these little dude cameras, right?"

"Yep. In the truck."

"Then I'll take this one since I'm used to it." She peered at Drew. "You okay?"

"Yep."

"Then I'm off to get me some shots of hot cowboys getting dressed for a wedding. Yeehaw!" She left the barn.

Drew smiled. She and Elise had grown up in the same household, but their personalities were completely different. Drew envied her sister's breezy attitude toward life. Elise had hated losing the internship, but she would have been okay, even without Drew rushing to the rescue. But Drew was glad her little sis was here.

She went to the truck to get a small tote and the other camcorder, and then she walked up to the house. Elise was right. Work was a blessing. Her gloom disappeared while filming Lexi getting into her classy wedding dress with the help of Chelsea and Philomena, her two attendants.

After everyone was dressed, Drew slipped into a bathroom and put on what she referred to as her wedding videographer's outfit. The emerald green knit dress with a gently flared skirt paired with low-heeled shoes gave her freedom of movement and the combination was appropriate for all seasons, including Christmas. Her pearl earrings and her grandmother's pendant were her only jewelry.

On the trip from the house to the barn, she met Elise coming back from her filming escapade in the meadow. "Have fun?"

"You know it, sis. Your guy is already down at the barn warming up his guitar, by the way. I'll meet you there after I change clothes."

"See you then." Drew wanted to get inside well in advance of the guests so that she could shoot the benches slowly filling up. During editing she'd increase the film speed for that segment. It wouldn't take up much of the video's runtime and it was a fun prelude to the big event.

Although Elise had prepared her by announcing Austin was already in the barn, her chest tightened with emotion when she caught sight of him. He wore what the brotherhood had chosen for the occasion—black pants and boots, white shirt, string tie, black Western-cut jacket and a black Stetson. His blond coloring with the dark outfit was breathtaking.

He glanced up when she came in and smiled appreciatively. "Nice dress."

"Thank you. Nice outfit."

"Thanks." He held her gaze for one electric moment. Then he went back to strumming his guitar.

She walked over to the corner where she'd positioned her tripod-mounted camera for maximum coverage of the event. She could swivel to the back to catch the action there and to the front for the ceremony itself. Elise would stand behind Cade with a handheld camera to catch shots from that angle.

Her hand trembled slightly as she turned on the camera and listened to the sound of Austin's guitar through her headset. She closed her eyes and took several deep breaths.

She would do this and she would do it well. Lexi and Cade deserved the best she had to give and she wouldn't allow herself to be sidetracked by her worry about the beautiful man over there playing guitar in the corner. But ignoring him wasn't easy when they were the only two people in the barn and she had nothing to do but wait.

Everything was as ready as it could be. She'd already taken video of the ribbons braided in each horse's mane and the flower arrangements hanging between each stall. She'd even filmed the gray tabby strolling through the barn.

The cat wandered over to Austin and rubbed against his leg. Austin stopped playing and leaned down to scratch behind the cat's ears. "Hey, Ringo. Don't know if you'll want to stay for this thing, buddy. Might be too big a crowd for you, but it's a big day for your main man, Cade."

"How's Cade doing?" She hoped Austin and Jonah had helped him relax. Most grooms were a little jumpy, but Cade had seemed more so than most.

"He's fine." Austin met her gaze as he continued to pet the cat. "Thunder Mountain guys are pretty resilient."

That was the exact moment she lost her heart for sure. It wasn't a wise thing to do but she couldn't help it. Austin had been through so much, and his courage in the face of adversity had touched her from the beginning.

She knew that for a man like him, love was a precious gift, one he didn't give lightly. They might not be meant for each other, but dragging out the uncertainty until tomorrow night wasn't fair to him.

She took a deep breath. "Maybe we need to have our talk a little earlier."

"Okay."

"Like after this is over."

"I look forward to it." His attention shifted to the back of the barn as the brotherhood filed in and positioned themselves shoulder-to-shoulder on either side of the back door. They were an impressive group. Austin tipped his hat to them. "Showtime."

And so it was. Drew filmed the guests as they arrived and were escorted to their seats by various members of the brotherhood. She had no trouble picking out Jack Chance and his mother, Sarah. For one thing, Finn introduced them to each of the brothers before seating them.

For another, they stopped to pet the horses on the way to their spots. She couldn't claim to be a horse person aside from her interest in wild ones, but she could recognize the signs. Jack and Sarah obviously loved them.

Curiously, mother and son didn't look related. Jack's chiseled features and dark coloring indicated Native American ancestry. Sarah was fair-skinned with Anglo features and the posture and height of someone who might have walked a runway in her youth. But they were clearly fond of each other and thrilled to be here. Thunder Mountain had taught Drew that biology wasn't the only component in mother-son relationships and maybe not the most important one.

As guests continued to arrive, Austin's gentle rendition of country songs filled the barn with nostalgia. Lexi had been right about using a solo guitar. This was far better than a sophisticated sound system and recorded music.

Damon and Finn ushered Rosie and Herb to a seat

in the front row. Drew glanced at the time and noticed that they were right on schedule. The same two brothers brought Lexi's mother to the front row.

Drew swung her camera to the back again as the rest of the brotherhood filed up the aisle. Several horses nickered as they passed. After all, these men were cowboys who at one time or another had ridden, cared for and loved those animals.

Finally the men reached the front of the barn and formed a semicircle with their backs to the open doors. Late afternoon sunlight streamed in, surrounding them with a golden glow. They looked magnificent and Drew took her time panning across the entire group.

Next Jonah and Cade arrived and took their places in front of their brothers. Jonah was dressed like everyone else, complete with the black Stetson and string tie. He looked more like a riverboat gambler than a man of the cloth.

Cade was the only one with a slight variation to the dress code. The vest he'd mentioned yesterday turned out to be gold brocade, and Drew's eyes misted when she saw it. During the time she'd filmed the women getting dressed, Rosie had given Lexi a gold locket from Cade along with a note explaining the significance of the vest he'd be wearing.

He'd bought it without consulting Lexi and intended it as a silent pledge of a long and lasting love. He planned to wear it again fifty years from today when they celebrated their golden anniversary. After reading his note, Lexi had burst into tears.

Once all the men were in place, Austin launched into a slightly more energetic song for the processional as Chelsea walked down the aisle wearing a delicate gown of turquoise. Philomena, dressed in a deep blue dress that matched her eyes, followed. She pushed a stroller covered in ribbons and flowers.

Sophie perched in the middle of all that finery wearing a crown of flowers and a frothy dress of apple green. She looked like a woodland fairy child, but she sounded exactly like the spirited baby she was as she squealed and bounced in the stroller. Cameras and phones came out and Phil's stepmother crouched in the aisle to get a picture head-on. Drew suppressed a burst of laughter when Rosie left her place of honor and did the same.

As Phil and Sophie took their places, Austin finished up with a flourish. Then he started a very simple version of a well-known melody and began humming it softly. The brothers behind him, including Cade and Jonah, joined in as the audience rose to the sweetest wedding march Drew had ever heard.

As the soft humming drifted through the barn, Lexi appeared on her father's arm. Drew had seen her outfit earlier, but the impact of it here was a hundred times greater. Against a backdrop of weathered wood, she was a glowing vision.

The classic, flowing lines of her white satin dress suited her perfectly. Cade's gold locket nestled at her throat, and instead of a veil, she wore a crown of white flowers over her short brown curls. Her bouquet was also all white except for a single red rose in the center.

The closer she came, the louder Austin hummed and the brothers took their cue from him. They almost drowned out the sound of Lexi's horse, Serendipity, who trumpeted her congratulations as Lexi passed by.

By the time Lexi reached the front of the barn, the brotherhood's chorus of deep baritone voices filled the space to overflowing with a joyous sound of celebration. Lexi obviously loved it. She alternated between tears

and laughter, which could be the sign of a perfect march
down the aisle.

Austin brought the song to a crescendo and cut it with
perfect timing. Silence reigned as everyone in the barn
absorbed the beauty of the moment when Cade and Lexi
stood gazing at each other. Then little Sophie called out
"da-da" and the spell was broken as everyone laughed.

Lexi's dad transferred her hand to Cade's and took his
seat, Jonah cleared his throat and the ceremony began.
Drew had filmed several weddings, but none had touched
her the way this one did. The love between Cade and Lexi
shimmered in the air, so real she almost believed it would
show up as waves of color on the video.

Her filming strategy was simple—stay focused on
the shining faces of the couple vowing to love each other
forever and a day. The words made Drew's throat hurt
but she didn't have time to question why. She was too
busy capturing a precious memory for two people who
deserved to have a video to play when that fiftieth rolled
around.

After it was over and they hurried down the aisle together to the vibrant tunes pouring from Austin's guitar,
after guests and members of the brotherhood had stopped
to compliment Austin on his playing, Drew found herself
alone with him once again.

Slowly he leaned his guitar against the wooden stool
and walked over to her. "You haven't ever asked this directly, but it's probably something you'd like to know."

She took a deep breath. "Okay."

"I want this." He gestured to the decorated barn. "And
I want it with you. My brothers would tell me I'm crazy
for laying it out, but…I saw how you reacted to this wedding. I don't know a lot of things, but after four years of

guiding trail rides I've learned to read people. I saw your face and I think you want it, too."

She opened her mouth to contradict him.

"Don't answer me now. Give yourself some time to think about it." He held her gaze. "Give yourself time to imagine how great we could be together." Then he glanced toward the back of the barn. "Hey, Jonah. Great timing, bro."

Drew stared at the preacher in confusion.

"Happy to be of service." Jonah tipped his hat. "All set?"

"Sure am." Austin looked at Drew. "Before he left I asked him to head back here after giving us a couple of minutes. He'll walk you over to the reception. On the way he's supposed to tell you what a great guy I am." Then he turned and walked out of the barn.

Chapter Twenty

Austin figured he'd blown it, but engineering that moment alone with Drew when the air still vibrated from the excitement of Cade and Lexi's wedding had been too good to pass up. She'd been so into it. Whether she realized it or not, she was a people person like him.

She had enough talent to create nature videos and could probably make money doing it, but filming people was her sweet spot. Building a wonderful life with her would be so easy, at least in his view, but she didn't think she was ready. Typical of him, he'd just pushed her to make a decision.

Good thing the rockin' party going on in the rec hall absorbed everyone's attention and no one noticed he was a wee bit distracted. Like all the other guys, he'd shed his jacket and thrown himself into the action—eating, drinking, toasting and dancing to the music provided by an excellent DJ. But his mind wasn't on the festivities.

Instead he was focused on Drew as she moved around the room with her small camcorder.

Cade was right about him—when he set his mind to something, he was exactly like a bullet train. Jonah had told him that he couldn't railroad people and that was what he'd attempted with Drew, pretty much from the beginning. Now she wouldn't even glance his way and it was his own damned fault.

The rec hall looked great, though. He hadn't seen the place when it was first built but from what he'd heard, it had been a bare-bones structure. Part classroom, part hangout for the academy's teenagers, it had been more functional than attractive.

The students had done a lot toward changing that. The walls were covered with murals, good ones, too. They'd created faux windows on each wall. One looked out on a startlingly realistic view of the Bighorns and another on a pasture with Thunder Mountain horses grazing in it. On either side of the front door, imaginary windows revealed a nonexistent porch lined with chairs.

While he and Jonah had been keeping Cade occupied this morning, the rest of the brothers had pitched in to decorate. Somebody had come up with colorful table-cloths, probably Rosie, but the guys had provided the vases of wildflowers on each table. They'd done a decent job with crepe paper streamers, too. The streamers added a high school prom vibe, but that wasn't a bad thing.

Maybe if he hadn't made his pushy speech in the barn, this night could have been a lot of fun. Drew would have stopped by during her filming and given him a smile. Later they could have slipped outside for a few stolen kisses. He could be wrong that she was deliberately avoiding him, but he didn't think so.

Then he saw her leave her camera with Elise and go out on the dance floor with Jack Chance. Okay, that did it. The guy was a great dancer and he'd taken a turn with nearly every woman in the room, but Drew was supposed to be working, right? And if she took a break to dance with anyone, he wanted to be the one holding her, not some well-heeled dude from Jackson Hole.

Making his way across the dance floor, he tapped Jack on the shoulder. "Cutting in."

"Oh, hey." Jack glanced at him without missing a beat. Then he looked at Drew and raised his eyebrows. "Okay with you?"

Austin clenched his jaw.

"It's okay." She didn't smile, though. Not even a little bit.

"I'll ask you again later. We need to catch up." Jack smoothly transferred her into Austin's arms.

He pulled her close, but not too close, and continued the lively two-step. "Catch up? You know him?" He didn't dare gaze into her eyes or he'd stumble. He was normally a good dancer but he was stretched tight as his guitar strings right now.

"I was his waitress once when he came to Billings to look at horses. He stopped by the restaurant for a bite to eat."

"How long ago?"

"At least five years, maybe more."

Austin's jaw muscles bunched. "Must have been memorable."

"It was. He danced me around through the tables."

"Sounds like quite a guy."

"Austin, he's married with two kids."

"Doesn't mean anything."

"In Jack's case it does. Listen, this is stupid. Let's go outside so we can talk."

He sucked in a breath. "That would be great." Taking her hand, he led her out the front door and into the cool night. "It's chilly out here. Do you need—"

"I'm fine." She faced him. "I've wanted to talk to you, but I wasn't sure what to say. I'm still not sure."

"You don't have to say anything." He shoved his hands in his pockets so he wouldn't reach for her. "Let me apologize for what I said back at the barn. Cade's warned me several times about my tendency to barrel ahead when I've set myself a goal."

"Your goal-oriented personality was one of the things I admired about you."

"You said 'was,' so I guess you don't admire it so much anymore."

"I still do, but what you want from me... I can't give you that. There's nothing wrong with having a plan but you need to find a woman who's ready for marriage. And kids. I assume you want those, too."

"Yes, I'll admit that I do."

"Austin, you've fallen for the wrong girl." Her eyes grew shiny with tears. "And I'm so sorry. I don't doubt your feelings are sincere. I'm...fond of you, too."

"Fond?" His heart cracked right down the middle.

"More than fond."

"Thank God. Drew, we can build on that. I promise not to push you. I'll—"

"But see, I already know what you really want. I've felt your urgency and even if you could dial it back, I'd wonder if you were mentally tapping your foot. On top of that, waiting around for me keeps you from finding someone ready and willing to fulfill your dreams. That's not fair to you."

"Don't worry about being fair to me."

"Can't help it." She smiled and swiped at her damp cheeks. "I really do care about you. I want you to be happy."

"Me, too."

"Then let me go. I'm not the person you need."

"You're making it sound hopeless."

"Because it is. Probably was from the beginning. We want different things."

He hit rock bottom. Since he had nothing more to lose, he decided to be blunt. "I still don't understand. Why are you so against committing to me, or any guy, for that matter?"

"Because I'd lose myself. It was happening in Billings—constant family obligations were distracting me and taking me away from my work. I felt scattered during a time when I needed to be focused on how to build my business. Moving here was a breath of fresh air, a welcome taste of freedom."

"It can still be that!"

"Not if I keep going out with you. I thought we could just have fun, but I realized fairly soon that you want more, plus you have a huge family, bigger even than mine." She took a shaky breath.

"Drew, I promise you they wouldn't—"

"If I became seriously involved with you and by association with your family, guaranteed the expectations would start up again."

"How can you say that? You've known most of them since June. Do they strike you as the kind of people who would do such a thing?" Frustration was a steel band tightening around his chest.

"I can't tell because I'm still mostly an outsider. Things change when you become part of the inner circle."

"I don't see it that way."

She sighed. "I know you don't because you love them. I love my family, too, but they're enough to handle without adding another larger group to the mix."

"You're making some big assumptions about how you'd be treated."

"They're assumptions based on hard-won experience. I'm sorry, Austin. It isn't going to work." She choked up on the last part. "I need to get back to filming." She turned and ran inside.

Disbelief and shock kept him where he was for several seconds. He hadn't even managed to open the door for her. All this time he'd thought if he handled things right he'd succeed. But he'd never had a chance.

When he looked at his family he saw warmth and acceptance, support and love. She saw a situation boobytrapped with obligations. He didn't have a clue how to fight that perception.

It seemed that her family had such a dynamic. He couldn't say because he'd only met Elise. Maybe Drew had felt a duty to bring her down here and cheer her up. But Elise hadn't pulled Drew away from her work. In fact, she'd rolled up her sleeves and helped.

Elise might not be typical of the Martinelli clan, though. Again, he couldn't judge without meeting more of them. But he sure as hell knew that his family didn't smother anyone with responsibilities that kept them from doing their work. Didn't matter. He could say that until he was blue in the face and Drew wouldn't believe him.

He'd made some mistakes in this deal, but even if he'd slow-played it the way Cade had advised, they would have come to this point eventually. Drew didn't think the trap would close until she'd officially become family, so she never would have agreed to be his fiancée, let alone his wife.

He wasn't good at accepting defeat, but this time he had to. At least there was plenty of beer inside that rec hall. That would be his solution for tonight. Tomorrow he'd work out a solution for getting over Drew. He knew in advance it would be one of the toughest goals he'd ever set for himself. Might even be unattainable, but he wouldn't know until he tried.

Elise's crush on Jonah turned out to be more of a blessing than Drew had counted on. Jonah was the big topic of conversation during the drive back to the apartment after the reception and Austin's name never came up. Jonah had also invited them out to breakfast the next morning but Drew begged off, citing the large amount of editing she had ahead of her.

She did have a ton of editing and she tackled it the minute Jonah picked up Elise and they took off. Getting through the rehearsal and the prewedding activities wouldn't be too bad, but she dreaded the footage of the wedding and the reception. Austin would be all through those portions.

Jonah brought Elise back from breakfast before Drew had made it past the rehearsal dinner, which was fine. No one would expect a finished product right away because there was so much. Monday morning she could work on the painful sections.

Elise continued to rave about Jonah on the way back to Billings. With her feet propped on the dash, she listed off all his sterling qualities. "I hope you meant what you said about visiting as often as I want because I'd like to take you up on it."

"Of course I meant it. You were a huge help this weekend and besides, I love seeing you."

"I love seeing you, too. I was sad when you left Billings so this'll be great."

"It will." So far Elise hadn't mentioned Austin. Drew wondered if her sister had sensed there was a rift and didn't want to bring up a touchy subject. That would be a relief.

"The main thing I like about Jonah is that he has his priorities straight." She crossed her ankles and wiggled her feet. "Does it distract you when I have my feet up here?"

"No." She smiled. "I'm used to it."

"Good, because I can relax better this way. Jonah thinks it's funny I do this."

"You put your feet on his dash?"

"Sure, why not? He says it's a working truck, anyway. No fancy muscle car or shiny new truck for that cowboy. He's considering buying a couple of horses, though. Austin asked him if he wanted to be a partner in his trail riding business. Did Austin mention that to you?"

"No, I didn't hear about it. Great idea, though."

"You should do a promotional video featuring both of those guys. Bet they'd get a lot of business from women if you did."

"Possibly, although I'm not sure I'll have time to make them a video." She'd forgotten that she'd offered to go on the first trail ride and film that, too. "I might need to recommend someone else."

"Why on earth would you do that when you... Uh-oh." She let her head fall back against the seat. "Wow, I've been in my own little world but now that I look back on it, I can see things weren't right. I thought you were just tired from all that work, but you and Austin had a falling-out, didn't you?"

Drew tried to calm her breathing. "Not really. We've accepted that we're not right for each other but it's not like we had a fight or anything. It's just over, which is for the best." That speech didn't come out as matter-of-factly as she would have liked.

"So he's looking for marriage and kids, after all?"

"He's looking for a wife who'll fit nicely into his big family. That includes having some grandkids for Rosie to spoil and I guarantee there would be a bunch of other expectations I wouldn't figure out until it was too late."

"What kind of expectations?"

"The same ones we have in our family—last-minute babysitting requests, whipping up an extra dish for the potluck because someone forgot to shop, acting as peacemaker for the family squabbles. You know the drill. I left Billings to get away from all that. Why jump right back into it?"

"*That's* why you left?"

"Yes."

"I thought it was because you got a job at the community college and you'd be closer to the wild horse refuge!"

"That's what I told the folks because I didn't want to hurt their feelings."

"Oh, Drew. I hate that you feel you had to leave because the family was stressing you out. I wish you'd told me."

"I didn't know how. You don't seem to have that problem."

"They bug me sometimes, and I'll probably end up moving somewhere eventually, but not because I have to get away from them." She fell silent.

"Look, I'd appreciate it if you didn't mention this to Mom and Dad."

"I won't. They'd be crushed."

"I know, and I love them both so much. It's just—I needed some space to figure out who I am and what I want. I don't know if I would have made that nature video if I hadn't left, let alone sold it. I really think that's my future, making more of those."

"Could be."

"Elise, I'm sorry if I upset you by saying all that. I don't hate our family or anything."

"Of course you don't. You wouldn't do all those nice things for them if you hated them. Hey, could we have a little music? I think better with music."

"Sure." Drew switched on the radio and punched the button to bring in a Billings station since they were within range now. She wasn't clear on what Elise might be thinking about but she'd be quiet and let her do it.

They were nearly at her parents' house when Elise spoke again. "Fortunately we're a couple of hours away from dinner and I have a plan. Dad will be taking his Sunday afternoon snooze and Mom will be catching up on back episodes of that show she likes, the one with zombies."

"She likes that?"

"She started watching it a few months ago and she's hooked. Go figure. Anyway, let's tell her we feel like climbing into the tree house to see what shape it's in."

"Why would we do that?"

"To see if it's fit for the next generation of kids. She'll buy it. I want to talk about this some more and that's the only place we can guarantee she won't hear us."

"I don't know. If she's watching zombie shows, anything's possible. She might decide to join us in the tree house."

"She might, but I'm thinking she won't. She's never liked heights."

Elise was right. Their mother had no interest in climbing up to the tree house and didn't think it was safe for them, either. But they promised her they'd test each rung of the old rope ladder carefully before going higher.

Drew insisted on going first. "I'm heavier than you. It'll be a better test."

"Okay, but if there are any cool spiders at the top, don't you dare kill them."

"Wouldn't dream of it." They'd both read *Charlotte's Web* and had never killed another spider since. Climbing the rope ladder brought back memories of lazy summers when she and Elise would haul a thermos of lemonade and a package of Oreos up here. They'd read sexy books they weren't supposed to have and talk about the day they'd unlock the mysteries contained in those books.

At the top of the ladder Drew glanced through the opening to the tree house their dad had built at least twenty years ago. "Lots of leaves and one small spiderweb in the corner," she called down. "Let me scoop out some leaves before you come up. Stand back." She climbed in and dumped handfuls of leaves out the door. Finally, she was satisfied. "Come on up."

Sitting cross-legged in her usual spot to the right of the opening, she waited for Elise to appear. She must have swung up that rope ladder like a monkey because in no time her head appeared and then she was in, taking her place to the left of the entrance.

She glanced around. "This is cool. I'm going to come here more often."

"We need to watch the time so Mom doesn't get worried. I forgot my phone."

"Then you really must be distracted. I brought mine." She pulled it out of her pocket and laid it on the dusty floor. "For starters, I want to make sure I understand. You broke it off with Austin because he wants to bring you into the bosom of his family and that freaks you out. Is that the basic idea?"

"More or less."

"What if I were to tell you that you have nothing to fear but fear itself?"

"I'd say you're quoting Franklin D. Roosevelt and it doesn't apply."

"Okay, but I need to say something. Don't get mad at me."

Drew laughed. "You always say that before throwing out something that's going to make me mad."

"And it probably will. Here it is. You're doing this to yourself."

"Doing what?"

"Getting tangled up in our family's problems, babysitting on short notice, making the extra potluck dish. You don't have to do any of that unless you truly want to."

"What are you talking about? It's expected!"

"That's true in your case because you always say yes. In fact, you usually volunteer. But, sis, you're allowed to say no. I do that a lot."

Drew gazed at her. "And you don't hear about it?"

"Sometimes I do. I just smile and say whatever they wanted from me doesn't fit into my schedule."

"I never considered doing that. What a startling concept."

"You're the oldest, so naturally you were conditioned to be the responsible one. I wasn't. It's easier for me."

"And you didn't feel you had to run away from home."

Elise reached over and wiggled Drew's foot. "In retrospect, that wasn't a bad thing. You met Mr. Gorgeous."

"You've been leading up to him all along, haven't you?"

"You know me too well, sis. Look, I was only there for the weekend so I can't say if his family is as needy or downright manipulative as ours can be. I'm guessing they're not, but who knows? The point is, you can hang with them and not give up your focus if you remember that you don't have to do what everyone asks, or suggests, or even intimates that you should."

"That would be completely new territory for me."

Her sister smiled. "Stick with me, kid. I'll teach you the ropes."

"The more you talk, the more I think my response to Austin was—"

"Knee-jerk?"

"Yeah."

"Hey, forgive yourself. And by the way, you're allowed to vote ixnay on the wedding and the babies for now. If he's not okay with that, then you really don't belong with him. But unless I missed something, he didn't give you a timetable."

She thought back over his little speech after the wedding. "He didn't, but I have the feeling he might have one. Besides, when I hear someone say *I want this*, I assume they mean right now."

Elise shrugged. "Explore that question with him, but I've seen the way he looks at you. I think he's open to negotiation and you're in a hell of a spot to strike a bargain that's good for you."

Excitement bubbling inside her, Drew scrambled to her knees. "I have to go back. I have to go back *now*."

"Then do it."

"I'll miss dinner with the folks." Then she laughed as years of obligation lifted from her shoulders. "But it doesn't fit into my schedule!"

"You're getting the idea, girlfriend!"

She crawled over to Elise and gave her an awkward hug. "I love you, sis."

"I love you, too. Now climb down that ladder. I'll be right behind you and back you up when you tell Mom you can't stay for dinner."

Drew was on the road to Sheridan in just under ten minutes. After her breakup speech to Austin, she had no idea what he'd be doing tonight. It wasn't even five o'clock, so maybe he wasn't drowning in his sorrows yet.

She tried never to make calls while she was driving, but this was an emergency. She grabbed her phone from the passenger seat and dialed his number.

He answered on the second ring. "Drew? Are you okay?"

"I'm *very* okay. I'm more okay than I've been in… forever! Listen, I want to amend some things I said last night. Can we meet?"

"Just name the time and place."

His firm, confident response sent heat spiraling through her. "My apartment."

"Give me directions."

She rattled them off. "I'll be there in less than an hour."

"See you then."

She broke speed limits all the way to Sheridan. She noticed a familiar truck in the parking lot. If she wasn't mistaken, it was Jonah's.

She hurried up the outside stairs and found Austin leaning against the wall next to her doorway. She'd kept her keys out because she didn't want to have this conversation in public. "I see you haven't bought a truck."

He smiled, and it was such a beautiful sight. "Couldn't get motivated."

"I thought a new truck was a priority." Her heart pounded as she fit the key in the lock and opened the door.

"Turns out it wasn't." He followed her in and kicked the door shut. Then he sent his hat sailing across the room and pulled her into his arms. "Tell me why you want to amend last night's comments."

"Because my brilliant sister pointed out that I don't have to let people load me down with commitments unless I want to." She felt a little dizzy from excitement but she pressed on. "She gave me a quick lesson in the power of *no*."

"Is that what you're here to tell me? No?"

"No! I mean, *yes*, but—" She paused to take a breath. "Austin, you really are like a bullet train."

"Damn it, I know. I need to fix that."

"No, don't!" She gripped his shoulders and gave him a little shake, although shaking a man built like Austin wasn't easy. "I love that about you."

"You do?" He gazed down at her in confusion. "I thought that was a big reason you broke up with me. I'm too intense. You think I'll railroad you into doing things you don't want to do."

"But don't you see what I'm saying? If I grow a backbone, if I stand up to you and tell you no, then you *can't*." She smiled. "I'll be bullet-train proof."

"That's a cute way to put it, but you wouldn't have to go through all that if I'd learn to dial it back."

"Don't you dare!"

His eyes widened.

"Don't you dare change that about yourself, Austin Teague. You go after what you want with a single-mindedness that not many people have. It's the reason you'll succeed at whatever you try."

"Are you kidding? I almost lost you!"

Love for him welled up inside her and tears pushed at the back of her eyes. "We almost lost each other."

He gathered her close and his gaze searched hers. "Please tell me we haven't."

"Not if you still want me."

His laughter was choked. "Want you? That doesn't begin to cover it. You're a part of me. I feel you in everything I do. I see you everywhere I look. I can't imagine life without you, but last night, when you said…" He swallowed.

"I was scared."

"Yeah, of me. Of what I'd ask of you."

She shook her head. "Of myself, although I didn't understand it then. Elise helped me figure out that I didn't have to do things on your timetable."

"What timetable?"

"For getting married. And having babies."

His cheeks turned pink. "You're right. I did have one."

"Thought so."

"I don't anymore. I'm learning from Cade's mistakes."

She'd thought she couldn't love him more than she already did, but that statement proved her wrong. Her throat tightened and she could barely get the words out. "Austin, I love you so much."

His breath caught. Then gradually his shocked expression changed, and like dawn breaking, warmth and light filled his gaze. When he spoke, his voice was roughened by emotion. "That's all I need to know." He cupped her face in both hands. "I thought I'd completely blown it and I'd never get to tell you this." He paused. "I love you, Drew Martinelli. I think I've loved you from that first day. You can call me an idiot, but I believe we're destined to be together."

"Then we're both idiots, because I believe it, too." And this time, when he kissed her, the world didn't disappear. Instead it expanded into a lifetime of adventure and love.

* * * * *

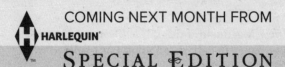

"Lydia Grant, assistant manager," he read, then lifted a
questioning glance to her. "Is that you?"

Her head made a quick bob, causing several curls to
plop onto her forehead. "That's me. Assistant manager
is just one of my roles at the *Gazette*. I do everything
around here. Including plumbing repair. You need a fau-
cet installed?"

"Uh, no. I need a wife."

The announcement clearly took her aback. "I thought
I misheard you earlier. I guess I didn't."

Enjoying the look of dismay on her face, he gave her
a lopsided grin. "Nope. You didn't hear wrong. I want to
advertise for a wife."

Rolling the pencil between her palms, she eyed him
with open speculation.

"What's the matter?" she asked. "You can't get a wife
the traditional way?"

Get 2 Free Books,
Plus 2 Free Gifts—
just for trying the Reader Service!

As soon as Zach had made the decision to advertise for a bride, he'd expected to get this sort of reaction. He'd just not expected it from a complete stranger. And a woman, at that.

"Sometimes it's good to break from tradition. And I'm in a hurry."

Something like disgust flickered in her eyes before she dropped her gaze to the scratch pad in front of her. "I see. You're a man in a hurry. So give me your name, mailing address and phone number and I'll help you speed up this process."

She took down the basic information, then asked, "How do you want this worded? I suppose you do have requirements for your…bride?"

He drew up a nearby plastic chair and eased his long frame onto the seat. "Sure. I have a few. Where would you like to start?"

She looked up at him and chuckled as though she found their whole exchange ridiculous. Zach tried not to bristle. Maybe she didn't think any of this was serious. But sooner or later Lydia Grant, and every citizen in Rust Creek Falls, would learn he was very serious about his search for a wife.

Don't miss
THE MAVERICK'S BRIDE-TO-ORDER
by Stella Bagwell, available September 2017 wherever
Harlequin® Special Edition books and ebooks are sold.

www.Harlequin.com

Reward the book lover in you!

Earn points from all your Harlequin book purchases from wherever you shop.

Turn your points into *FREE BOOKS* of your choice
OR
EXCLUSIVE GIFTS from your favorite authors or series.

Join for FREE today at
www.HarlequinMyRewards.com.

Harlequin My Rewards is a free program (no fees) without any commitments or obligations.

MYR17